The Stone Lions

By Gwen Dandridge

Published by Hickory Tree Publishing
HickoryTreeBooks.blogspot.com

Library of Congress

ISBN: 978-0-9893157-8-4

NSF grant 9552462

The illustrations have been modified for the black and white issue of this novel. The original color ones may be found at my Web site at www.gwendandridge.com

Book Design by
Cover Design by Carol Heyer
Back cover and spine by Sherrie Petersen
Illustrations by Carin Coulon

First Hickory Tree Publishing Edition

Acknowledgements

Certainly this book would never have been thought of, much less created, without the generosity and inspiration of Dr. Dorothy Wallace at Dartmouth. The National Science Foundation's support was much appreciated.

Anne Lowenkopf was the person who made this book happen. She believed in both me and the story, and kept me writing the many times I would have given up. My greatest wish is that she were alive to see it published.

Many thanks to Dr. Sarah Tolbert for explaining band symmetry to me over and over until I understood it and even began to love it. And to her and Dr. Ben Schwartz for all the walks we took discussing plot and math.

Josh Schimel, my husband and love, who has stood by my side the whole time, ever willing to listen, critique or support.

Judith and Michael Thompson, who patiently read revision after revision. Heather Latham and Robert Hill, who took photos of every illustration from the Owen Jones book on the Alhambra. Carin Coulon for her work creating the illustrations. Rebecca Finley for her massive support.

Antonio Orihuela Uzal, for his help and his book, *Casas y palacios nazaries,* about the Alhambra during the late 1300's.

My writing group with Val Hobbs, Sherrie Peterson, Kim Hernandez and Lori Walker who pushed me to rework *The Stone Lions* one last time.

Sonia Connelly, Bob Orser, Teri Davis, Claire Beorn Norman, Pippa Drew, the Medieval ListServer, Yuki Yoshino and so many others who have been important to this book's birth.

The original fountain from the Court of the Lions is depicted on the cover. It was stolen in the 1500's and replaced with the lower fountain that now resides there.

Chapter 1

Granada, Spain – Early 1400's, Alhambra Palace

Ara pulled her brown cloak tightly around her head as she risked peering out between the sun-dappled leaves. She had chosen this spot carefully for its thick shrubbery and its great view of the Justice Gate at the south entrance to the palace. There was barely enough space to hide a slender twelve-year-old girl—and it even let Ara see part of the road leading to the Alhambra, the Red Palace. Any moment the mathemagician might appear, and now Ara would be among the first to see her arrive.

Ara gnawed at her ragged thumbnail, thinking again of Suleiman's reaction if he were to find her not only outside the safety of the harem, but outside the palace as well. It was hard having a tutor who watched your every breath.

The Sufi mathemagician, Tahirah, though she was but a woman, was one of the most important scholars in all Islam—the same Sufi who had instructed her mother in mathemagics and symmetry when she was Ara's age. And Tahirah was arriving now. *Oh, to see her arrive, not just to hear others tell, but to see the procession herself.* She knew Suleiman would fault her for being too curious yet again.

Ara rechecked her position—she must stay totally still while the procession came through.

Not far off, a trumpet blared. Ara jumped. "Still as a mouse," she reproached herself. Again the trumpet sounded. Booming drums announced the approach of the mathemagician. Horses whinnied and tossed their heads, jingling the silver bells on their reins. Ara held her breath as the procession crested the road. First came palace guards in blue, gold and white uniforms, their faces fierce as they marched four-by-four at the head of the procession. Two men with thick arms carried a red and gold banner embossed with the symbol of their tribe. Next, garbed in their billowing, white Bedouin caftans, came the honor guard astride their legendary desert horses. From her shelter, Ara strained for a sight of the mathemagician.

Where *was* she?

The parade continued, dust swirling around the horses' hooves. Ara's nose twitched; she fought a sneeze. Slowly, so as not to attract attention, she brought her hand up to cover her nose. Too late.

"Achoo." She froze, panicked. If she were found outside the palace walls far beyond the safe haven of the harem—and not just *any* girl, as her tutor kept telling her, but the sultan's daughter, alone and unprotected—she would be in trouble.

A palace guard turned but never looked deep within the bushes where she sat, still as night, robed in brown and green. One more searching glance, and he turned back to the procession. Ara shivered in relief.

Her eyes widened at the sight of the elaborately dressed slaves bearing the litter of the Sufi mathemagician. The Sufi's companions, concealed beneath the muted indigo hijabs of the mathemagician's clan, walked alongside. Behind them followed more veiled women in sand-colored robes, their hands clasped and heads bowed, honoring Allah. The horsed guards came next, followed by three more litters. Trailing these, dozens of Sufis from the whole of Granada followed in hope of seeing the visiting scholar.

Ara held her breath, knowing the price she might pay for her curiosity if she were caught. But if even half the wonders whispered about the mathemagician were true, the wise woman would have the power to transform Ara's life. The curtains within the gold litter slid aside. It seemed to Ara that violet eyes met her brown ones, laying bare all her secrets. *No one can see me,* she reassured herself, no one — certainly not through the silk curtains of the litter. The litter passed, and the parade moved toward the grand steps of the palace, but for Ara the moment of connection with those eyes remained.

At the top of the steps, Ara's father, splendid in his robes of state and flanked by his principal advisors, waited to welcome his guest. Three of his wives stood behind him, veiled in black hijabs. Only their eyes showed, as was fitting in so public a place.

Abd al-Rahmid, the wazir, stood off to the left, his mouth pulled down in its usual scowl. His eyes scanned the peacefully assembled crowd. *He always looks grumpy when there is no one to bully*, thought Ara.

The curtains of the litter were pushed aside, and a woman stepped out of the carriage, her hair wreathed by a white shawl. Her handmaidens quickly moved to assist her.

Why, she's tiny, Ara thought, *almost as small as my cousin, Layla*. Again, Ara felt violet eyes watching her—although Tahirah never turned in her direction but walked with poise to Ara's father.

He smiled and bowed. "Welcome, kinswoman. You grace us with your presence. We hope your stay will be long and enjoyable, *inshallah*— if Allah wills."

The tiny woman bowed in return. "Allah is gracious in allowing me to visit your fair city, *alhamdulillah*—praise be to Allah." She tilted her head slightly, her shawl moving with the gesture. "It is long since I last saw the countless beauties of the Alhambra Palace and enjoyed the hospitality of the Nazrids." Her hand gestured toward the mountains. "Word comes even in the far reaches of the world that you continue the enlightened rule of your father and his father before him. The honor is mine." The Sufi bowed her head with the grace of a queen.

Ara heard her father reply, "I am proud to call you kinswoman, however distant." He gestured to the hijab-covered women. "My wives have requested the privilege of escorting you to your rooms in the Palace of the Partal. I could not refuse them so great an honor." He smiled again, concern edging his eyes. "But you are weary from your travel. Rest—and when you feel renewed, I hope you will give a small talk on symmetry or a reading of poetry."

Tahirah nodded, her eyes meeting his. "I would be delighted to do so. But you are right. It has been a trying time."

One of her father's wives—Zoriah, Ara guessed, noting the erect posture—spoke quietly to the Sufi. Zoriah turned back to her sisters-in-marriage.

If only my mother still lived, Ara thought, *she also would be standing there.*

The women conferred softly before quickly taking the traveler to her lodging.

Ara watched the crowd dissolve through the Gate of Justice into the walled palace, going their separate ways to baths, servants' quarters, and stables. The wazir stayed until all were gone. Ara glared, willing him to go. What was he waiting for? Every minute he stayed, she was more likely to be missed. She shivered. The image of her petite, graceful cousin drifted before her, disapproval and alarm radiating from gentle brown eyes as she'd listened to Ara's plan.

Ara closed her eyes and pleaded to the heavens. *As Allah is kind, don't let Suleiman ask Layla where I am.*

The wazir remained, pinning her to her hiding place. Abd al-Rahmid glanced around furtively, making sure he was alone. Searching the folds of his caftan, he retrieved a shiny metal rectangle. He scanned the plaza again.

Why the secrecy? Sunlight flashed against the metal; a ray of light glinted on its edge. Moving quickly, the wazir grabbed a small frog that had been cowering beneath a bush. The light seemed to disappear, and then *two* frogs dangled by their legs from his hand. He turned the metal over twice and rotated it once in a circle, all the while chanting. Darkness gathered where he stood. Ara jumped as she heard a slight pop and one frog vanished. Blood dripped from the wazir's hand, and a foul stench drifted across the courtyard on a small gray cloud.

Ara's stomach churned. The wazir looked around again. He tossed the remaining frog into the bushes before carefully wiping the gore from his hand. A thin smile reached his lips; he pocketed

4

the piece of metal within his sleeves and strode through the palace gate.

Ara frowned as she crouched in her hiding space. What had he been doing? Near where he stood, a small portion of wall seemed to twist.

She thought for a minute. Was this something she should tell her father? She frowned again. She'd have to confess she had been where she was forbidden to go. Besides, what would she say? That she didn't like the way he smiled? That the wazir killed a frog? Maybe he didn't like frogs. A lot of people didn't, she recollected, thinking of her aunt.

Still, she considered, staring at the spot where the frogs had appeared, blood darkened the floor. It felt very wrong. And it looked like magic.

Chapter 2

Ara waited some minutes to make sure it was safe to emerge from her hiding place.

"Harrumph."

Ara whirled and stared at the large, corpulent figure, vibrating with anger, now peering over the hedge.

"A worse charge I never had," Suleiman hissed, his nose flushing red in agitation. "A disobedient, thoughtless, willful girl-child who frightens all who care about her with her foolish curiosity." The tip of his tall hat bobbed with each word. "I'm grateful that your mother, Allah's prayer and peace be upon her, isn't here to see you brashly standing *outside* the palace gates with no protector and"—he looked at her more closely—"covered with dirt and debris." Suleiman pointed an offended finger. "What if you were taken, Allah forbid, by an evil Christian?" he continued, glancing over his shoulder as though one might leap out from behind a tree.

Ara wrinkled her nose. "Christians don't come to Sufi processions. And they probably don't have any use for Muslim girls," she added as an afterthought.

"You say this, knowing the People of the Book are sniffing at our borders!" Suleiman gasped. "The sultan has warned that our lands are desired by the Castilians. Look at you, beyond the safety not only of the harem, but also of the palace. Some in the harem are already so worried by your wildness they push to find you a husband." He raised his voice as if uncomfortable with this possibility.

"Let us go now and show the sultan how his seventh-born obeys. He will not be pleased that one of his household disobeys his directives." Suleiman's hat slipped forward slightly, and he pushed it impatiently back into place.

Ara winced and bit her lip nervously. Marriage? She needed time to explore and learn and question. Soon enough she would be an adult and tied to the harem, but not yet. How could she explain how important it was for her to see the Sufi arrive? "Suleiman, I'm sorry you worried. I just had to see her. I *had* to," she whispered. All too vividly, she envisioned her father's disappointment and anger were he to find out. She bowed her head in shame and beseeched, "No one saw me; please, don't tell Father." Suleiman hesitated, studying his young charge. "*Please*," she whispered again.

Suleiman didn't answer, but stood gazing down at her. He seemed to grow even taller in the awful silence. Then his voice boomed out, "Translate one hundred pages of the Koran into Spanish, and I may—just may, depending on how good the translation—be too busy reading to go to your father with this latest misdeed."

Ara flinched. A hundred pages! That would take days. But at least her father would not be told. "Thank you, Suleiman," she replied meekly.

"But remember," Suleiman warned, "one more transgression..."

"Oh, no, Suleiman. I will be very good, truly I will." But even as she spoke, Ara knew she would keep trying to discover a way to reach the mathemagician. It couldn't be wrong to wish to sit at the feet of the heroine of the old tales, one of the great minds of the century. Ara glanced up; Suleiman stared at her intently, and she looked back as demurely as she could.

He eyed her suspiciously, but the tip of his hat bobbed again—though with less force than before. "The girl child shows some thought, however little, about the feelings of others. Perhaps there is hope of your learning to listen and obey." His nose was slowly returning to its normal color. "The women are asking for you to play for them, while your cousin Layla huddles by the fountain looking like a kitten cornered by a badger." He sighed as he led her toward the palace entrance. "Quickly, we must get you inside and tidied up before further damage is done."

Chapter 3

The mathemagician walked in a daze. Led by the four wives of the harem and followed at a discreet distance by her guards and handmaidens, she carefully reached out and explored the palace walls. Her head spun. Danger! She could feel it in the core of her being: the magic of the Alhambra was being defiled.

"We're so pleased to have you visit," one woman commented.

"You are too kind, *alhamdulillah*," Tahirah replied, trying to keep part of her mind on her hosts. Dark emotions whirled around her, buffeting her with fear and pain.

"This time of year is lovely with the scent of orange blossoms in the air," another put in politely, pointing toward the heavily perfumed trees.

Tahirah nodded courteously, trying to appear interested. "The Alhambra gardens are what legends are made of."

It was difficult for her to keep up a conversation while also probing the destruction of mathemagical symmetries within the walls. The Alhambra's protections had been tampered with. She placed her hand casually on one embossed tile and felt the agony seep into her body. Sweat broke out on her forehead as the pain flowed through her.

"Are you ill?" someone asked anxiously as Tahirah sagged, weakly wiping the sheen of perspiration from her forehead.

This was not something to tell, not until she understood it further. Tahirah gathered herself before speaking. "It has been a long day and, while I am grateful for your company, I am no longer young. I need to bid you good day so that I might rest from my journey."

"Of course. How thoughtless of us." Zoriah clapped her hands twice and the litter-bearers rushed to her side. "Please take the scholar to her rooms in the Palace of the Partal. See that she has whatever comforts the Alhambra provides."

The women clustered together, watching anxiously as their guest was borne away.

Inside her small litter, Tahirah leaned back in exhaustion and contemplated the danger. The Alhambra's magic was still holding together, but it was being pried apart layer by layer. Soon, if nothing was done, the bands of magic would stretch too tightly—then snap.

Once she reached the privacy of her chambers, she dismissed her guards and handmaidens, closing the door firmly behind them. She removed her white cloak and, folding it with trembling hands, laid it across her bed. Beginning at the door, she walked slowly around the room, fingers exploring the walls, checking carefully for any spell set to catch the unwary. Stopping occasionally to listen, she continued her slow, methodical search. As she completed her circuit, she breathed a sigh of relief. No danger lurked here. Still, she knew she must place sacred protective formulas in the room before she rested.

Carefully, she chanted the words and placed each magical ward—two at the door, four at the windows, and one in each corner of the room. Stars of gold, green and silver glowed before disappearing as each ward was set upon the framework of the Alhambra.

She yearned for sleep, but rest was not possible until she had sought out the cause of the Alhambra's pain.

Tahirah cleansed herself ritually in the way of the Sufi, preparing for the ordeal to come. She sat in the middle of the room, murmuring formulas, and slowly entered the realm of magic. Little by little she opened her mind to the palace, and there she drifted, inviting communion.

Nothing was as it should be; the fortress was breaking. Small fissures formed deep within the structure—but during her attempts to heal it, the very walls recoiled. She turned her mind to the Court of the Lions and called, once, twice, three times, listening for the lions to respond. But only her voice echoed back.

Hours later, she came to herself, lying stunned on the floor. The Alhambra had rejected her, fighting her and her magic, divulging nothing.

The Alhambra had been betrayed and trusted no longer.

Despite her powers, she had been unable to heal the breach. The palace cried out for help, yet rebuffed her attempts. How could she begin to heal this?

Except for her slow, even breathing, all was silent as she puzzled over this. Who had done such a thing—and why? From whom would the Alhambra take comfort? Not from an outsider or one with foreign blood, that seemed certain. The Alhambra had closed herself off from all but those born on her soil.

Tahirah stared at the ceiling, hoping for answers. Finally, as the evening drifted into night, she gathered Allah's truth and power once again and prayed unto Him for guidance.

Chapter 4

Ara tried to look repentant as Suleiman barked at the servants to finish tidying her. Every so often, he glared at her as if she might disappear before his eyes.

"Can you not be faster?" he snarled to the woman dressing Ara's hair. "They are waiting for her."

Su'ah finished plaiting Ara's hair but remarked with barely disguised disdain, "Perhaps if a certain eunuch had not been toying with being a mathematical scholar, he might not have mislaid his charge."

Suleiman's voice choked with fury. "I do not toy! Symmetry is important to all who are Islamic." He huffed and glanced with slitted eyes at Ara. "And my charge was not mislaid," he snapped. "She was merely not at hand."

Ara rolled her eyes and thought of the many places she would rather be. Still, her interest pricked up. This was the math that her mother had loved. The teacher her mother had loved. She leaned over the window, looking out at the latticed view. The wazir strode by, his hand touching the walls, stopping to look closely at the designs that covered them.

Maybe symmetry had something to do with what the wazir was doing. If I understood mathemagics, I might understand what he did with the tile and the frog.

"At hand? This is Ara we're speaking of, not a coin. You are too distracted by mathematics to be in charge of this child's learning."

Ara jerked back to the conversation.

Su'ah's eyes sparkled with malice as she continued baiting Suleiman. "Perhaps one child is beneath a Turkish eunuch's notice. Especially a Turk who desires the position of translator for the sultan."

Ara's head came up. Now there was *really* going to be a fight. Suleiman looked as if he were about to burst; the tip of his hat jiggled so fast it seemed to dance.

"Suleiman, as you have said, we must go," Ara said quietly, walking over to him. She grasped his hand and gently pulled him toward the door. "Please, would you get my lute? I do not wish to keep them waiting any longer." Suleiman turned his head from Su'ah to Ara. She could see his desire to have the last word warred with the pressing need to get her to the Court of the Lions.

As soon as she arrived, Ara saw Layla curled miserably in a corner, clad in her dancing dress. The courtyard was walled on all sides, but above was only the blue of the Andalusian sky. Women were arranged like flowers around the central fountain. The rich embroidery of their clothing complimented the elaborate patterns that decorated every surface. Stone tiles covered the floor, and the surrounding garden of jasmine, orange trees and roses spilled onto their edges. Blue and red patterned carpets lay strewn across the floor, while twelve stone lions stood guard around a huge central fountain. Water flowed from the lions' mouths into narrow channels that trickled off to other rooms.

Nine-year-old Hasan lay on his stomach as he floated a small wooden boat in the stream. His younger sister Jada clapped with glee as it spun past her. Servants and slaves moved about, offering tidbits of food, rubbing oil on bronzed skin, and fanning two women seated upon brightly colored cushions. Above them rose narrow, graceful columns that supported the sculpted arches of the courtyard terrace.

Three other women sat off to the side, playing a game with dice and small round disks. Maryam, one of the game players, frowned slightly as she glanced at her daughter, Layla. Other children sat with their mothers or played quietly by their sides; nursemaids hovered nearby.

"There you are, Ara. We've been waiting forever for a musician. Layla, stop sulking and dance for us," the sultan's fourth wife, Dananir, told the girls.

Ara hadn't thought she could feel any worse—until she saw the look of pure relief on her cousin's face.

Layla rushed forward to hug her. "I was so very worried," she whispered. "Everyone kept asking and asking where you were."

Zoriah observed Ara suspiciously. "We looked for you all afternoon, and you were not found. How could that be?" She raised one eyebrow.

"Play 'The Hidden Treasure,'" Thana called to her. "It's such a lovely tune." Others chimed in, "Yes, please play 'The Hidden Treasure.'"

Thanking Allah for the distraction, Ara moved to the fountain and affectionately patted the rough stone mane of her favorite lion. Ara could sense Zoriah's eyes upon her as she tuned each string of her lute. As usual, once Ara began playing, the day seemed brighter and her worries drifted away. The water rushing through the statue sounded much like the purring of a cat. Legend told that the fountain was magic and that in times of danger the stone lions would come to life, rising to defend the Alhambra. Ara smiled, envisioning the water-spouting lions protecting the palace.

She relaxed as she picked out the familiar melody. Layla removed her blue caftan and started the steps of the dance. Each motion fluid and sure, she stepped through the complicated rhythms. She swirled around and around, every muscle trained to move as she wished. Three younger girls twirled, their arms over their heads, in imitation of her. Ara, who had no talent with her feet, greatly envied her cousin's grace.

When the song ended, Layla and Ara looked into each other's eyes and grinned.

"Play another," requested Dananir, smiling up from the cushion where she sat holding her youngest son. "That was lovely."

Even Suleiman, standing by the arched doors, seemed relaxed and pleased.

Shadows deepened as the afternoon wound to an end. Servants walked around to check the candles and tapers set along the walls, and the crowd began to disperse. Suleiman walked Ara back to the harem quarters in the Palace of the Myrtles.

Ara looked up and gave him her best smile. "Suleiman, would you teach me a bit of plane geometry? My calligraphy and French are getting better, and you even said I'm pretty good at math."

"Mathematics, not math!" he corrected automatically. "Is this the way you make amends? By teasing those who watch after you?"

"No, truly. I want to understand symmetry. My mother studied it, did she not? Is it true—is symmetry the cornerstone of Islamic art?"

Suleiman snorted in amusement. "So that's why you disobeyed? You wish to follow in your mother's sandaled feet?" He shook his head. "Ah, yes, symmetry is central in our art, it's the foundation of our architecture, one of the great logic mysteries that our people have unfolded." He waved his hand, encompassing the whole of the Alhambra. "Look around you. The whole of this fortress is covered with art, and most are symmetries." Ara stared in wonder as she looked about her. Suleiman stooped low, pointing to a wall decorated with a row of triangles in line with Ara's eyes. "It is simple. Symmetry is merely the repeating of pattern. The trick is to find the pattern." He encircled a triangle with his hands. "See how this triangle is repeated, as if a mirror were held at its side."

Ara looked at the triangles on the wall. "Yes, I see it, but it's only two triangles, why is it important?" she asked, turning her head sideways to better look at it.

"Because," he told her, "it's a pattern. Look with both your mind and your eyes. Here." Impatiently, he grabbed her hands. "Hold your hands out in front of you, thumbs together. Are your hands the same?"

She looked at them. "Oh, I see! It's as if I held a mirror next to one of them and the mirror reflected the other."

"Yes." He smiled, the tip of his hat nodding in easy agreement. "You have to imagine there is a straight line between two objects that you 'flip' either object over—where you would place a mirror. The flip, or reflection, is called a *motion* in symmetry. Here—let me show you another example: let's look at handprints." He dipped his hands into a nearby fountain, then crouched down and made a row of handprints across the stone floor. "You copy me," he enjoined. In less than a minute, two rows of handprints marched across the floor, one large and one small.

"See, with these handprints, each flip moves you farther

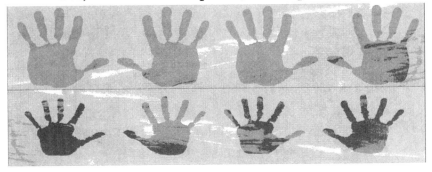

along the row. Band symmetry is used to describe flat things, like prints or tiles." He smiled suddenly. "I'll get you a small mirror. That is the best way for you to understand reflection or mirror symmetry. If you wish me to teach you more about symmetry, you must find three examples of vertical reflection motion in the Alhambra. You're a clever girl. It should be easy for you. When all three are found and *correct*, we will continue, yes?"

Ara puckered her brow at the mention of a mirror. The disturbing image of the wazir crossed her mind. Had the shiny metal been a mirror? Was he merely studying geometry? Again she wished her mother lived. She would have known.

Another thought occurred to her. What would happen to the Alhambra if the symmetries changed? She opened her mouth to ask, but Suleiman continued.

"You understand? Each symmetry must be *perfect*."

The tile that the wazir had stood in front of couldn't have been perfect before he was there. Tile didn't change like that; it was made from ceramic. That would be magic.

"Ara! Are you woolgathering again?" He frowned at her. She looked up from the pattern of the quickly drying prints and grinned as she flicked water at Suleiman.

"Could a tile change? Change what it is?"

"You *are* woolgathering." He sighed. "No, that isn't possible. If you were to find a tile that would change what it is, then you might well believe that I too could change what *I* am."

"But what if it did?"

He snorted. "Then I too will change, my fanciful child. But let us try to deal with what is possible, shall we? Find the symmetry."

"I understand. I can do it," she assured him, grinning in amusement.

"Remember," he rebuked, painstakingly wiping the water from his nose, "all the symmetries you need are *inside* the Red Palace grounds: the Palace of the Lions, the Palace of the Myrtles, the Palace of the Partal, the guildhalls, the gardens, the fortress, the mosque, and the stables. You must never again go outside the gates of the Alhambra."

"I won't. I'll only look inside the palace walls." Ara stared at her handprints. "I think I see what you mean about this symmetry, but won't you show me the others now?"

A few heartbeats passed as Suleiman seemed to mull over Ara's transgressions of the day—then, with a visible sigh, he gave her shoulder an awkward pat. "You do very well for a girl-child. I will teach you symmetries again, but now it's time for sleep."

Ara looked at him seriously. "Promise? You won't forget?"

"I promise. There are seven band symmetries, vertical reflection which you just learned, horizontal reflection, double reflection, translation, rotation, glide reflection and glide with a vertical mirror. I will teach you all of them." He drew himself up proudly. "I am a Turk of the Qizilbash tribe. Our word is our honor. And even were I to forget," he continued, smiling, "a certain girl-child is sure to remind me."

Suleiman turned to leave, and Ara's smile faded as her eyes noted a twisted and warped tile on a shadowed wall. But by then Suleiman was far away, too far to call. Besides, it was only a tile. Nothing for her to worry about, and nothing to do with the wazir.

Chapter 5

"Father," Ara called, leaning over the balcony, "is the mathemagician going to lecture today? Could I come hear her if she does?"

"Ah, my littlest scholar." The sultan left the pool edge. Ara ran down the stairs to the Court of the Myrtles. Her father picked her up in a tight hug. "You have grown, my treasure. Almost too heavy for me to carry."

"I grew two fingers-width last month. I'm almost as tall as Su'ah now."

He put her down and smiled appraisingly. "So you are. In answer to your question, Tahirah is resting. She comes here for a time of peace and renewal, and the trip was more exhausting than expected. When she does give a talk, I also hope you can attend.

"Your teachers praise your skill in the classical studies. However, they were less moved by your obedience and grace." He grinned at her and ruffled her hair. "Still, I am pleased, my daughter. I prefer a curious mind to a lazy one. Allah himself, blessed be His name, praises learning. As He has said, 'To seek knowledge is required of every Muslim.' Your mother would have been very proud," he added with a sad smile.

Ara waited, hoping he would say more about her mother, but nothing came. It never did.

"Come, join me. I'm going across the palace to the orchards and would love the company of a pretty lady."

"Could I? Are you not too busy?" she asked, thinking of the days he spent closeted with his advisors over boundary disputes. She had overheard Zoriah and Maryam whispering together about their fears for the fragile peace between Granada and Castile. Two months ago, three murderers had been hanged at the Justice Gate. Her father had overseen the trial. Lately, she heard, he had been making trade agreements with the countries to the north: Aragon, Navarre, Castile and France.

The sultan sighed, gazing vacantly at some unseen trouble. "Yes, my responsibilities press on me. I keep hoping my affairs will settle down, but, *Insha'Allah*, if it is Allah's will." He shrugged his shoulders and smiled. "But today I'm fortunate and have time to spend with one I love. Walk with me. Let us enjoy the morning." He reached out his hand.

Together they strolled along the cobblestone pathway from the Palace of the Myrtles into the gardens, where a pair of hawks circled, screeching encouragement to a young hawk learning to fly. Ahead was the *Generalife*—the Summer Palace. The road led outside to the *Cuesta de los Chinos*—the Path of the Stones. The *Generalife* was set behind the Alhambra on a higher hill sheltered on three sides by the mountain itself.

After a brisk walk up the hill, they entered a long tree-shaded corridor. To Ara's right was the dark green of the pine forest, and on the left the orchards and vegetable gardens overlooked the Alhambra proper. Her father moved his Court up here during the hot summer months when cool breezes would catch the tops of pine trees with the whisper of mountain air. She and Layla would sit telling stories in the *Patio de la Acequia*—the Garden of the Canal—and play hide-and-seek in its many gardens.

From the orchard, the view went on forever. All this was her father's domain and her father's father's before him. All the way to the Mediterranean Sea, she was told. City after town after farm, thousands of people relied on him for trade and safety.

She glanced up at her father as they walked. *He looks weary, and his beard has much gray in it.* Still, she noticed, *I must trot to keep up with him.* She knew he missed her brothers and sisters, who had gone away, one by one, to other lands. Her elder brothers were at universities in Persia, training so they could rule as wisely as her father. Three of her sisters were married, far off in worlds ruled by sand and sun. Even if she looked as far as she could, she couldn't see where they were. And no amount of wishing and dreaming would bring her closer to exploring those countries. Those lands were beyond her reach—even beyond the snow-capped mountains of the Sierra Nevada in the distance.

Below her nestled the Alhambra. Onward to the west, the *Vega*—the great plains—rolled out until they ran smack up against the mountains. Her father's world...and hers.

In the town below, she could see the church of the People of the Book, the Christians, with its tall steeple and the bell that rang out every Sunday. It seemed odd to her that no voices of the muezzins sang out five times a day, to call the Christians to prayer.

"Father, are the Christians evil?"

He looked at her sharply. "What brought this on?"

"Suleiman was worried about the Christians, that's all," Ara hedged.

The sultan looked out across the *Vega*. "These are hard times," he explained. "But there are good and bad people in all religions. Christians, Jews, Muslims, no one group has all of either. Right now, many Christians want us out of Al-Andalusia—Spain, as they call it—and that makes it hard for us to be friends.

"You remember Father John, the kind priest you met. He's a good man. There are those who are not as kind, and we must be wary of them whether they are Christian or not. We are fortunate to have the harem. No man can cause harm there, so our loved ones are protected. It's the law for Muslims. It's a comfort to me to know that my children, wives and grandmothers are safe."

Ara looked at him doubtfully.

"You have no reason to worry. Suleiman looks after you, and the Alhambra is a very great fortress." He bent down to her level. "Is that what's troubling you?"

"But why do they want us out of Al-Andalusia? The Nazrids have ruled here for hundreds of years."

"It's true. We Muslims have been here a very long time, almost seven hundred years," he responded sadly, looking across to the mountains. "But many of our cities and fortresses have fallen. We have given much to our world, but Granada is the last of the Muslim countries in all of Al-Andalusia." His voice dropped as if he were speaking to himself. "Our neighbors continue to press into our borders."

"Is that why you always look so worried?" Ara asked.

He stopped short, staring beyond her for a minute before replying. "We are in a time of change, and we must ride that change as best we can." A look of sorrow crossed his face before it was wiped away as if it had never been there. "The Alhambra protects its own. It is a wondrous fortress, as beautiful as a woman, and protected with powerful magic. As long as we hold true to our honor, the palace will stand, *inshallah*."

He seemed to shake off his dark mood. "But you shouldn't be bothered with such things. Keeping us strong and at peace with the People of the Book is my job, not yours." He patted her shoulder, and then looked about as if something were missing.

"But I want to help."

"Ara, you're a girl. You need to study the lute, read poetry and grow into a lovely, learned woman, not stand in my shoes." He winced when she ducked her head at his obvious annoyance. "Come, let us not disagree. Look at the gardens. Have you ever seen such a beautiful sight?"

She looked out across the field. Beyond, at the edge of the forest, a movement caught her eye. The wazir, looking much like a bat with his brown caftan whipping around him, stood huddled in conversation with two men. Not Muslims, Ara decided, assessing their clothes and odd hats; perhaps soldiers from Castile or Aragon. She thought again of the wazir's bizarre ritual at the Justice gate, still unable to make any sense of it.

One of the foreign men saw them and pointed. The wazir whirled and noted his observers. Then, abruptly dismissing the men, the sultan's chief advisor strode purposely toward Ara and her father.

Hurriedly, Ara asked, "Father, is there something bad about frogs? I saw..."

He sighed, and she felt as if she watched him change from her understanding father into the sultan. Doubt and distrust showed in his eyes as he observed the men across the way. "Not now, child. There are those with whom I must speak. In a few weeks, new tribute agreements must be signed. I must consult with my advisers and negotiate the details. Let me get the guards to walk you back to the palace."

Chapter 6

The soft lilt of a tune woke Ara to the morning light stretching across her room. Su'ah was humming quietly to herself as she arranged clothes on the shelf. Ara's gold-embroidered, beet-red vest and saffron-yellow pants that tied at the ankles lay next to Layla's gold-green caftan. A silver-inlaid tray filled with olives, cheese, bread and steaming mint tea sat on the table near the window. Ara could feel Layla curled next to her like a sleeping cat. *Probably dreaming of dancing*, she mused sleepily and, from the warmth of the bed, watched Su'ah shuffle around the room. *Su'ah was old*, she thought, observing her through sleepy morning eyes. *She cared for my mother and Layla's mother when they were babes, and now she does the same for us.*

Both she and Layla had been born twelve winters ago. Ara's mother had died from childbed fever soon after. Her father, it was said, had deeply mourned the passing of his learned Egyptian wife. Su'ah had been given the care of her and, later, that of her cousin when Layla's mother, Maryam, had become sick with grief over the loss of her sister. Layla's father, the sultan's younger brother, had comforted his wife as best he could, and finally, Maryam had regained her health, strengthened by the love of her husband and her joy in her newborn child.

"You awake?" Su'ah slowly moved across the room. Her slave tattoo was faded in the wrinkled creases of her cheek. "After morning prayer, you two should head for the baths; the day awaits. It is said that the Sufi scholar may come here this evening to speak. I hear that she is rested and working on some mathemagical problem or such."

Ara pushed off the wool covers and jumped out of bed, stubbing her toe in the process. "How can two cousins be less alike?" Su'ah exclaimed. "A tidy, obedient girl who dances on air, and a reckless, too-curious child who cannot walk without bumping into walls."

Ara sat down and held the throbbing toe. "Father says I learn quickly and have a scholar's mind," she said in her own defense.

"Ara is brave and smart and daring," Layla said, stretching slowly in bed. "She knows three languages and is not afraid of anything."

"She would do better to know one language and learn to watch her tongue," the servant retorted. Su'ah then turned to Ara. "The sultan is far too lenient with you, child. You have almost the same training as a boy. You need to get your head out of the clouds and down to our own Allah-blessed earth. Suleiman is not the best person to be educating a gently bred girl."

Ara knew these arguments well. She remembered when Su'ah had caught her learning to fight with a quarterstaff. And then, of course, there was the time she had climbed to the top of the Tower of the Children to better study the stars. At least she hadn't fallen far.

Layla gave Su'ah a disarming smile. "We are fortunate to have both of you to watch over us. Allah is good."

Su'ah sniffed. "It is fortunate, indeed, that *I* am with you, else you would run as wild as gypsy children. Here, Ara, let me comb your hair. I'll not have it said that you are unkempt as well."

Layla and Ara soaked in large baths as, in the dim light, steam from the hot water rose to escape through star-shaped holes cut into the ceiling. Other women and children were there also, quietly bathing. Some sat on stone benches, drying themselves. One of the concubines' toddlers was crying, indignant at having her face scrubbed. Hasan and two other boys had been splashing water back and forth but were stopped abruptly by a fierce look from an older servant. A slave poured water over Dananir's hair, while another moved to gently knead perfumes and oils into her skin.

Layla stared at her fingers under the water. "Ara, would you help me search for my ring? I know I had it yesterday, but I can't find it."

"Your little gold ring with the amber stone?" She dipped her head under the water for a final rinse. "Your mother gave that to you for your eleventh birthday, didn't she?"

"Yes, and her mother's mother gave it to her when she was a girl. I took it off to dance and put it on my caftan, but it's missing," Layla said.

"Perhaps it fell while you were dancing. We could look in the Court of the Lions. And while we're there, I can look for more symmetries. Suleiman says that I must find examples of the symmetry named vertical reflection before he will teach me the next symmetry. I've already found one right here in the baths."

"Oh, show me," Layla exclaimed, looking at the many decorations covering the walls.

"See? There on the wall near where Dananir is sitting." Ara pointed. "The gold leaf that repeats over and over in a line, see how each set of leaves are sort of reversed?"

Layla studied the design for a few seconds. "Yes, but how do you know it is a vertical reflection symmetry?"

"Suleiman told me the design had to be in a row, and that each pattern had to be exactly the same shape and size." Ara ticked off reasons with her fingers. "And you need to pretend there is an imaginary line between them that they can flip over. If you could flip each tile, it should match exactly on top of the one next to it. Suleiman promised to teach me more as soon as I find all three examples."

"But how do you figure out where the line is?"

25

"Suleiman said it is a vertical line." Ara held up her hand with fingers tightly pressed against one another. "So, I look at a tile and pretend there's a line that goes up and down—straight down into the earth and up into the sky to Allah. I try to see if the design on the tile can be split in half. If it can, I fold the two parts together in my mind to see if the designs match."

They finished bathing and climbed out of the waist-deep water, then slipped on their sandals set at the edge of the pool. Hot water piped under the floor made the tiles too hot for bare feet. Ara was careful to put her sandals on. She had pretended she was a mystical firewalker once when she was six, only to blister her feet for her effort.

"Well, *I* don't think a woman should flaunt herself," they heard Fatima remark primly from around a corner. "Or her education. Tahirah runs around the world doing who knows what. She needs to be under her brother's control. A woman should be a thing of beauty, not have her nose forever in books. Why, only yesterday, I heard the wazir say he thought a woman scholar was a disgrace to our people and a bad example to the children. Worse, she's a Sufi, with no regard for *our* ways."

Ara scooted closer, sticking her head around the corner and peering through the handle of a large urn overflowing with flowering pomegranate branches.

Rabab chimed in. "There's nothing wrong with being a Sufi. They love Allah, as do all good Muslims. Only they follow their hearts, not the words of any person." She looked around for agreement.

Dananir spoke up softly. "The prophet Mohammad said 'God does not look at your form.' Allah doesn't care if one is male or female."

Maryam, Layla's mother, added, "A learned mind is praise to Allah. He, in his wisdom, admires education."

Rabab leapt in again. "Our wazir, Abd al-Rahmid, is still angry because he was sent home in disgrace from the university. You'd think he would have gotten over that by now—it's been

26

close to two decades. The man is forever looking for someone to belittle. But for his counsel, Suleiman would have been named head translator. Look how he sulks because that Sufi woman is here. Tahirah is a famous scholar, and Abd al-Rahmid's a bitter, jealous man." Several women murmured in agreement.

Dananir spoke over them, "Suleiman is the palace tutor because the sultan needed one he could trust to teach his children. Anyone can translate a message."

Never easily derailed from her subject, Rabab plunged on again. "And then there was the fuss over Maryam—don't you remember, Fatima? The wazir petitioned the sultan for her in marriage."

There was a gasp from Maryam, and Layla looked at Ara in surprise.

"You remember, dear?" Rabab added. "You practically begged the sultan not to betroth you to him. It did work out well, though. Our sultan's brother, Abn al-Humam, has been a wonderful husband to you." There was a stunned silence before Rabab continued, lowering her voice. "Besides, I heard the wazir dabbled in the dark mathemagics."

Zoriah sent her a sharp glance. "We will not bring up past hurts, and we will not speak evil of anyone. Not Tahirah, who is an honored guest of the sultan, and not Abd al-Rahmid, who is the sultan's appointed wazir and, as you know, a trusted advisor. The sultan does not take kindly to the slander of his people.

"Unless you have proof of wrongdoing, we will speak of this no more. As it is said," Zoriah went on, "'the Ways to God are as numerous as the breaths of humankind.' We all have our place in the Alhambra. The wazir as advisor, Suleiman as palace tutor. In the harem, it matters not what the wazir thinks—this is our place. Allah, blessed be His name, and our sultan wish women to learn. And we shall obey their wishes," Zoriah finished decisively, her position as the sultan's head wife clear in her tone.

Ara and Layla sat stunned until the women left. "I didn't know the wazir offered for my mother or that he was sent home disgraced," Layla whispered.

"I didn't either," she whispered back, thinking of the dead frog. "What I want to know is, what are the dark mathemagics?"

Chapter 7

"I'm sure that I took it off here," Layla said as she circled the area for the tenth time, her eyes moist with welling tears. Suleiman stood talking to two servants on the far side of the large room. He turned his head toward them every few minutes, unwilling to be a target for Su'ah's sharp tongue again.

The two girls had retraced Layla's steps again and again. *She is so careful*, fretted Ara. *It's my fault she forgot her ring. I know how much she worries. I shouldn't have told her I was going outside the palace walls.* Ara moved to her pet stone lion and wrapped her arms around his neck while Layla sat down to think.

"What if it fell into the channels of water?" Layla leaned forward onto her elbows scanning a channel. "It would be lost forever."

Ara hesitated for a moment, thinking of the narrow channels that led away from the fountain. "Well, the water could push a ring downstream. Maybe the water moved it to a different room, or perhaps it was swept outside into the drains."

"But where? The Palace of the Lions is huge, and the channels lead to many places. If it went outside, we would never find it." Layla rubbed her eyes, obviously trying hard not to cry.

"I bet we could follow the water's flow and see where the ring might have gone if we put some dye in the water," Ara suggested.

"Oh, no." Layla sat up. "No good would come from this. Remember what happened with the soap. You had to scrub floors for a week before anyone would speak to you."

"That was a long time ago. I was only eight," Ara said dismissively. "I'm sure it would work. I'd just use the least little bit of dye. It would be gone before anyone noticed. It's springtime— no one is inside much. They're either in the Palace of the Myrtles or outside in the gardens telling stories and reading poems. By the time they come inside, the dye will have floated out of the palace and we will have found your ring." Her favorite of the stone lions made burping noises as the water bubbled out his mouth. "Even my lion agrees."

"I don't want to get into trouble," Layla commented uneasily. "I worried so when you were outside the palace gates alone."

Ara said nothing.

Towing the bucket alongside, Ara chuckled to herself. It had been hard getting the dye, what with Suleiman's watchfulness. Days had gone by before he was called away from Ara's side, and then no one seemed to be dyeing clothes. But now, after two weeks of searching, she had it.

"This bucket is heavy," Ara muttered to herself. She moved it to her other hand. The rope handle kept digging into her palm, and the dye sloshed around ominously, threatening to tint her clothes a merry beet-red. *I won't be missed until evening prayer. Suleiman's off teaching Dananir's eldest—and besides, he thinks I'm studying in the far garden.*

She was pleased with herself because she had found one more reflection symmetry in the Court of the Myrtles, red and green flowers arranged across the wall. Sure enough, she could see that each flower could be halved exactly. And by flipping over each half, the pattern would repeat across the row. *Find the pattern, you find the motion,* Suleiman had said. She sat down to rest by the side of the palace. *Soon, he would have to keep his promise to explain another symmetry.* She checked her left palm for blisters. She picked up the bucket and continued wending her way through the palace rooms to the Court of the Lions. After some thought, she followed one channel far upstream past the Hall of the Two Sisters.

Just a little, she told herself, as she carefully held the pail of dye to the edge of the channel. *Only the least little bit. That's all I need to track the water.*

Trumpets blared from outside the walls, announcing visitors. Ara jumped, bumping her knee against the bucket and spilling masses of beet juice into the water channel.

"Oh!" She watched in wide-eyed dismay as the red dye rushed down the waterway. Behind her she heard a roar, and she spun around, but heard nothing more.

The red dye flowed on. Nothing could change what had happened. Nothing would make it disappear.

"Bread and water for a month," she moaned, gritting her teeth. *That's what will happen to me if Father or Suleiman finds out.*

"Maybe it will disappear before anyone sees," she muttered without much hope. Dragging the incriminating bucket along, she trotted after the crimson water as it wound through the corridor, into the Hall of Two Sisters, down to the Court of the Lions. There it flowed out of the lions' mouths into a basin surrounding the fountain to head out again in three more directions. Twelve stone lions surrounded the fountain, just as always. Nothing moved but the ever-present trickle of water.

Ara hoped it wouldn't hurt her lion to spit dye. Ruby water spilled into the four channels, and she decided to look first in the Hall of the Abencerrajes. The channel ended in the center of the square room, where the water spilled into a low round fountain. Above the fountain was a golden eight-pointed star that filled the ceiling. Sunlight poured though arched windows along each of the star's edges and, in that dancing light, the lions almost seemed to stir behind her. She circled the low fountain, checking for a small gold ring. Nothing. She shivered, looking at the red dye that now filled the fountain. *It almost looks like blood.*

All the channels ended except one—there, the red water finally tumbled over a small ledge and into a drain near the Garden of the Lindaharaja. Ara sat down behind the bushes, frustrated and discouraged. An insect buzzed her ear, and a small pebble poked her knee.

The whole morning searching, and no ring found. Instead, she was certain there would be trouble over the dye. As the water trickled by she wriggled uncomfortably as the stone bruised her. Where could the ring have gone? As she leaned forward, the pebble poked into her knee again. Annoyed, she reached under her leg to throw the annoying pebble as far as she could. A glint of metal caught her eye. She brushed aside the dirt and grass to expose a band of gold. Layla's ring! It must have bounced off the wall and rolled away as it went over the ledge. She grinned and placed it on her finger.

The unexpected shuffle of soft-soled shoes on the garden's cobblestone walk caught her attention. She peeked between the branches of the bushes. The wazir again! Ara watched closely, scarcely daring to breathe; his back was to her as he stood in the entrance of a small room tucked into the side of the palace. Shadows clung to him like birds of prey, and Ara thought of Rabab's words. Was Abd al-Rahmid an evil mathemagician? As he opened the door, the glint of many tinned mirrors caught her eye from the room beyond. He turned slightly, and she could see that he again held a mirror—only this time it was a lizard that flailed in his other hand.

She couldn't quite make out his words as he turned and rotated the mirror.

One lizard became two, both now lying stunned in his hand. He swiftly dropped one lizard on the ground and stepped on it, crushing its head. The other he flung into the bushes. The tiles on the side of the door writhed. Ara rubbed her eyes. That wasn't possible. The walls of the Alhambra *couldn't* change pattern, and yet they were. Her stomach turned as she watched the tiles move.

The sameness was gone; the four tiles on the wall no longer matched. The fourth tile was tilted and curved in on itself, as if in pain.

Ara shut her eyes against the impossibility. A stench of smoke burned her nose as its gray cloud crawled by. When she opened her eyes again, the wazir was gone. She crept from behind the hedge and examined the tiled wall. There had been identical patterns before the wazir chanted—she was positive of that—and now they were different. *This can't be right*, she thought. *I must not be remembering correctly.*

She backed away and stowed the bucket behind the bushes before racing toward her rooms. With each step, Ara debated what she had seen. And with each step, she became more unsure. *If I tell, Zoriah will say I am bearing tales.* She wrinkled her brow as she thought about the problem. "I'll tell Suleiman. He'll know what to do."

"Su'ah," Ara called, "have you seen Suleiman?"

"There's no need to shout," Su'ah said. The shuttle of her loom moved steadily back and forth. "I'm not deaf yet. He and Layla were looking for you." She stopped her work. "They couldn't find you in the garden. A girl-child has a talent for disappearing, it seems," she added with a purse of her lips.

Ara frowned. "But I need to speak with Suleiman."

"Why should one such as I know the mind of a Turk?" Su'ah sighed, then tapped her fingers against the front beam of her loom. "He can't be far, though I heard he may be leaving in a few days on an errand."

Ara wiggled her sandaled toes in impatience.

"You're a mess again," Su'ah remarked abruptly. "Your hair needs rebraiding, and there is dirt on your face." She rose to get a hairbrush and a sponge. "Does studying require you to roll on the ground? Or do you—is that blood on your cheek?" she asked anxiously.

"Oh. No, it's just a crumb of food." Ara hurriedly wiped at the splotch of beet juice. "I'll go find them," she said, anxious to be off.

"Always hurry and rush," Su'ah scolded, fussing with her hair. "You should slow down, be more like your cousin. That child is a pleasure to care for, calm and orderly. Her clothes are always neat and folded—not strewn about as some I won't mention. You're looking a little flushed, child. Did you get too much sun, or are you coming down with a fever?" She placed her hand on Ara's forehead, then nodded, assuring herself. "Just too much fun, I think.

"The call to prayer is soon. It's nearing twilight. Don't forget your prayer rug," Su'ah admonished as Ara rushed off.

Chapter 8

Tahirah felt the palace shudder. Someone was practicing black mathemagics. Symmetry was being pulled from the Alhambra's walls, and the palace seemed closer to its breaking point with each change. Every day she saw subtle hints of evil as she walked through the gardens: tiles twisted, garden pathways slightly offset—but most of all, an unsettled feeling within the walls.

She had kept to herself these few weeks, hoping to discover who was creating this havoc. Through prayers and fasting, she gained a murky glimpse of the wrongdoer, but never a clear image. The palace's protection was its magic, hidden in the symmetries and inscriptions that covered wall after wall. If many more symmetries were destroyed, the Alhambra would fall. And if the Alhambra fell, Granada would fall, and Islamic Spain with it. Tahirah recoiled at the images of war and bloodshed that washed over her, and she uttered a silent prayer. She must uncover the culprit. The evil must be contained.

The building called out in pain as it twisted and turned in on itself. Again and again, Tahirah came upon an unexpected asymmetry. A corner would whisper of crooked lines as she passed, a ceiling would murmur of warped beams. The stone lions must know, but they were silent. They stood as guardians of the Alhambra—fierce, incorruptible and steadfast. There was no sign of one standing by the sultan. How could he govern without a lion by his side?

She called to them, and their silence was more ominous than any roar of rage.

Meditation and prayer had told her the key to repairing the damage was tied to one born in the Alhambra. But who?

She recalled the hidden presence she had sensed days before, a girl teetering on the edge of womanhood. Was she one whom the Alhambra would trust? Could she be entangled in this?

Perhaps she should take an interest in the girl. Would that put her at risk to the evil? So difficult a problem.

Tahirah sighed—time to put this aside for the moment. The sultan had asked her to join him and his household for a reading, and she must not delay. The sultan seemed pleased with her request to meet in the Court of the Lions. For all its beauty, she had another reason for going there. If the Stone Lions would but speak with her, she might be able to resolve the danger quickly.

Four palace guards arrived outside her chamber. As soon as she had covered her hair, her handmaidens ushered them in. She took her place among them and walked toward the Palace of the Lions. She planned to read some of Rumi's poetry and, perhaps, one piece of her own. A small discussion about the wonders of symmetry and geometry would round out the afternoon.

The sultan and his court joined her at the entrance. His wives and many children were waiting for her, but none of these stood out as the key that would unlock the Alhambra's mistrust. He dropped back to speak with the wazir and two other advisers. More of the harem's eunuch guards came to take their places along the walls, vigilant as always. A troop of servants followed, carrying trays of pomegranates, olives, artichokes, roasted goat and lamb. Rugs and cushions had been placed about for the comfort of all. Blind musicians played in the background.

The Court of the Lions was lovely in any light. In the early morning, it was the color of lavender honey. Now, with the stars glittering in the sky above and torches lighting the side walls, it was bathed in orange and gold. In the Hall of the Two Sisters, it was written, "The stars themselves long to spend their time in the Court of the Lions," and well could she believe it. Though the room was muted by the evening sky, she could see the lions standing frozen around the center fountain where the waxing moon's glow danced on the splashing water. She moved closer to read part of the inscription around the fountain: "He who beholds the lions in menacing attitude, knows that only respect for the Emir contains their fury." *So*, she thought, *they are ready.*

She stepped around the fountain, passing a portly slave; Suleiman, she recalled.

All of a sudden, a woman gasped, startling Tahirah out of her thoughts. "Blood," a woman screamed. "Blood on the lion's chests." Another took up the alarm, crying. "Evil has come down on us."

What were the women shouting about? No blood had been shed here. She would know instantly. The eunuch guards leapt to attention and milled about in search of an enemy. Mothers gathered their children and stared in horror at the fountain. The sultan stood his ground.

"What's this?" the sultan inquired, frowning slightly, as he stepped over to the fountain to peer into the red-streaked water. Tahirah stuck her finger in the water, rubbed it against a dark red line of grout before placing it to her mouth. She smiled. "Beet juice, it seems. Not blood."

"Beet juice?" repeated Suleiman, his clothes indicating status of some importance. As she watched, his hat teetered on the verge of falling off.

At the edge of the group, a girl with big, gentle eyes clapped her hands over her mouth. Layla, wasn't that her name? Suleiman pulled Layla to the side, mouthing the words "Where's Ara?" to the girl. Whatever she replied had him turn and abruptly depart.

"This is merely a mistake," the sultan soothed. "Not blood, just dye. There is no cause to worry."

Tahirah watched the rest of the people. The wazir had moved away from the crowd to pace anxiously around the room. Now, he walked up to one of the other advisors, and after a brief conversation, he also left the room. The women grew calmer—some even laughed.

The sultan turned to Tahirah. "Please excuse this disturbance. Someone must have accidentally spilt dye in our water upstream." He glanced toward Layla and frowned. "It would be carried through to here. No harm has been done.

"Perhaps you would tell us a story, a simple story, from Scheherazade's *The Book of the Thousand and One Nights.* I think no one could fully appreciate poetry or geometry just now." He smiled and almost casually strode over to Layla, engaging her in a conversation.

Tahirah sat on a cushion. The black-enshrouded women and brightly clothed children gathered about her. The sultan, his men and servants stood beyond that circle. "Sire," she began, "there was once upon a time a fisherman...."

Chapter 9

Ara stared at the door. How many times had she been told that "Curiosity is a trap for the unwary?"

It was early evening when Ara returned to the garden. She had not found Suleiman or Layla. She stood before the wazir's room, examining the tiles that surrounded the door. They had been identical, she was sure, but now each one was slightly twisted from the one below. They had become warped. What could have caused that?

And then there was the wazir. Maybe something in his room could explain his odd behavior. She wouldn't be spying, exactly. The door was closed. Girls were not permitted to open closed doors, but how was she to understand the wazir without entering? She hesitated, then gently pulled the doorknob. *If it's locked, then I wasn't meant to go in.*

The door opened easily with a slight creak, and she stepped in. What she saw was amazing. Mirrors filled every wall, and every single one was cracked or broken. Her astonished face was repeated in mirror after mirror, broken by fractured lines that distorted and reflected her image, twisting it, again and again. On the floor and the ceiling were spirals that seemed to swirl as she stared at them. A profusion of glass jars stood on a shelf, holding many small dead animals.

Ara turned slowly around, watching as her fractured image followed. A mirror image of triangles and circles wavered across her vision. *Symmetries*, she thought, her stomach reeling as she looked about. An elaborate tapestry-covered screen stood in the right corner of the room portraying a hunting scene with dead and dying animals. The dank air in the windowless room made her head feel funny. Torqued geometric shapes repeated in the mirrors before her: squares and triangles and circles. Her head throbbed.

I don't like this place.

The door swung open and then slammed shut. Heart thumping, she spun around.

"There you are. What trouble are you..." Suleiman stopped in mid-speech; his face turned a pasty white as he looked around the room. The mirrors now reflected two astonished faces. "No," he gasped. "Not the evil that repeats." He grabbed Ara's hand, tugging her frantically toward the door. "We must leave here now." Too late! Both heard the sound of approaching footsteps.

"Hide, quickly," Suleiman whispered. "Don't move. Say nothing." He shoved her behind the tapestry screen as the door opened with a snick.

Ara froze in shock behind the screen as the wazir spoke, his voice sounding like rough stone, "On whose word are you here in my room uninvited?"

"No one's. I..."

She heard the scrape of a sword pulled from its scabbard, and Ara clamped her hands tightly over her mouth so she wouldn't scream.

Even from behind the screen she could hear the venom in the wazir's voice. "You're spying on me! You've been too interested by far in my doings, stepping into what you shouldn't."

"No! I'm not...the door was ajar. I was concerned, nothing more."

"I can see it in your eyes, you want my magic. You can't have it. It's mine." His voice rose. "I've worked too hard for this."

"Please, for Allah's sake, for your own, let us leave here. Come, it will be well, no one will know."

The wazir laughed. "You're right. No one will know, and no one will heed your disappearance. You ran, back to Turkey. Another slave gone. Yes, you're no longer a difficulty for me."

Ara listened, horror-struck and terrified.

"You must not do this. It's evil. Turn back before you yourself are lost. Allah is watching."

"You threaten me, you who are lower than low!" The wazir laughed, a grating noise with no joy. "The answer is here. You will be tied to this palace forever. Chained to the symmetries themselves."

Ara remained locked in place while Suleiman pled. The wazir began chanting again, just as he had with the frogs. Ara heard a loud gurgling pop and then the wazir's shrill laugh.

"How fitting and fortunate. The blood of a servant of the Alhambra will speed the Alhambra's doom. And you, you will crawl on your belly until you die. Should I kill you or let you live a hopeless life in your new form?"

The call to evening prayer sounded. He laughed mockingly, "Perhaps Allah Himself has spoken and granted you a reprieve. Farewell, lizard. I must attend prayer or someone might notice and wonder." The door slammed.

Ara closed her eyes tightly and silently prayed to Allah that Suleiman would call to her. Only silence answered. Finally, she inched sideways to look around the screen. Suleiman's clothes lay in a heap on the floor, and a dark puddle of blood stained the tile. Ara shuddered, then started as the tip of Suleiman's hat moved. As she watched, a green lizard crawled stiffly out from under the pile of clothes.

"No," Ara murmured, pushing herself back against the wall. "This did not happen."

I'm not really here. I'm out in the garden sleeping. I'll wake and tell Layla this dream, and we'll both laugh. Please, please, let me be dreaming! Any second Suleiman will come for me and tell me to go inside for the evening meal.

Onto her lap crept a plump lizard with a crest that shivered in the air. "Oh, Suleiman, what am I to do?" The lizard looked up pleadingly at his mistress and curled into a tight miserable ball.

Run. Return to the safety of the harem before the wazir returns, a voice inside her head compelled. *Run.* Violet eyes, so like the ones she had seen at the Sufi's arrival, seemed to urge her. Ara gathered her courage.

Her hands shook so hard she could barely tuck the lizard into her caftan hood before tensely peering out again from the screen. All that remained were her own shattered reflections. She ran to the door and eased it open. The garden was empty. She leaped out of the room and raced for the palace doors.

Once safe in the sleeping room, she huddled in a corner, cradled the lizard, and sobbed.

Chapter 10

When her tears had finally evolved into black despair, Ara lay in her bed, numb with shock. She gently soothed the still stunned lizard before settling him carefully back in her caftan hood. Night came and, with it, the normal life of a harem. People moved through her room getting their bedding and preparing for sleep. On her finger, Layla's ring was an undeniable reminder of her folly.

"Child, what is wrong? Are you ill? I was told you were sick and in bed." Su'ah leaned over Ara and anxiously stroked her hair. Layla hovered beside her, nervously stepping from one foot to the other.

"I have a headache," Ara responded listlessly. She wished they would go away. How could she explain all that had happened? Suleiman was a lizard because she had misbehaved. The tears rolled again.

"You're crying," Su'ah stated with alarm. "What happened? Did you get into trouble? Are you hurt?" She sat on the edge of the bed and checked her charge's forehead.

"My head aches," Ara repeated. *Why won't they go and leave me alone?* "I just want to sleep."

"I knew you were coming down with something. You shouldn't have gone traipsing around this evening." Su'ah tucked the blankets around. "Why, you're still in your caftan. Let me help you off with this."

"No, please." Ara feared for the lizard in her hood. "I'm fine. It's only a headache. I'll get undressed in a minute. Please, Su'ah, get me some mint tea. I think that will help me feel better."

"Of course, dear. Let me go find a kitchen servant and order you tea. I'll be right back. Layla, maybe you should sleep with me tonight. I don't want you and the other children catching this," Su'ah added over her shoulder as she left the room.

"Ara, can I do anything?" Layla asked quietly.

43

From beneath the covers, Ara pulled the ring from her finger and handed it to Layla. "I found it. Please, go away. I don't want to talk. Can't everyone leave me alone?"

Layla stared silently at the ring in her hand.

Ara sat up, suddenly alert to the difficulty of hiding the lizard Suleiman in the harem. "Wait," she leaned toward Layla. "You *must* promise to tell no one," she whispered, reaching into the hood of her caftan.

"Tell what?" Layla leaned over to listen. She jumped and gave a little yelp when Ara held out the lizard. "What are you doing with that lizard?"

Ara choked. "I can't tell you—but you must promise that you will hide him very, very safely. He must be protected from any harm. It's so important, Layla. Please do this for me," she pleaded. She clutched Layla's hand. "Su'ah mustn't find him, and you must tell no one. Promise!"

"I promise," Layla wrinkled her nose at the lizard and reached for him carefully. "Will he bite?" she asked.

"No, and he won't run away. He needs food and water. I think they eat bugs. Tomorrow, I'll be able to take care of him, but if I keep him here tonight, Su'ah will find him for sure."

"What's Suleiman going to say when he finds out you're keeping a lizard in the palace?"

Tears threatened to roll down Ara's cheeks. "He's gone. Don't say anything to Su'ah or Father until I tell you."

"Suleiman ran away?" Layla whispered in disbelief. "He wouldn't! He loves us."

"He didn't run away," Ara sniffed. "Su'ah's coming back. I'll tell you tomorrow. Please, just don't say anything, not about Suleiman and not about the lizard."

Chapter 11

Tahirah, attended by her handmaidens, walked steadily forward into the Hall of the Ambassadors. She was uncomfortably aware the weakness had magnified in the walls of the Alhambra during the previous night. Inside her sitting room, a single tile within a vertical reflection twisted. Nothing she tried would remedy it.

Right before that occurred, she had seen a dark gloom of evil hanging near the sultan's daughter, the one named Ara.

Tahirah's head still throbbed from the waves of aftershock. She stopped after entering the Hall, waiting upon the sultan's command, and he acknowledged her entry with a nod. As she moved into the room, the light that twinkled through the stained glass ceiling hit her eyes like a shard of that same glass.

At the far end of the room sat the sultan, the neutral expression on his face belying the tension in his body.

He raised his hand in a vain attempt to rein in the sharp-voiced woman beleaguering him, then lowered it to the throne in disgust.

Fatima didn't appear to take notice, "It's as I said last year," she told him. "You can see that I was right. I say this for the child's welfare. She needs to be taken in hand before it's too late. She runs around out of control. She frightened us all with blood in the channels." She nodded to reinforce her conviction. "A diet of bread and water, perhaps, would drive home the anguish she inflicted on me. I mean us."

Tahirah remained in place. A harem dispute was being brought before the sultan. There must be much discord among the women for this to happen.

Fatima glanced around for approval as she rambled on. "It's time to find her a husband. There's no reason to put this off. I was married at ten, and Ara's a full two years older."

The sultan, who had been absently drumming his fingers throughout, looked away as if attempting to gather his patience.

Zoriah shook her head at Fatima and exchanged an anxious glance with Maryam. "Beet juice. It was only red dye."

The sultan nodded and spoke with great restraint to the older woman. "I want to thank you for bringing this *again* to my attention, Fatima, but, you will recall, she is my daughter." The room was silent. "I will decide when it is time for her to be married and to whom."

He softened his words. "Ara does need to be more aware of the effect her behavior has on others. While I am displeased that she has been cause for concern, it was only dye. Ara will clean the *dye* from the lions." His emphasis was another reminder that the stain was not blood.

Tahirah used her magic to seek within the room's deepest recesses for his lion. It was as she feared: his lion was not at his side, nothing that anyone would notice but a Sufi mathemagician.

"It was all very upsetting," Fatima added, not the least troubled by the difference between dye and blood. Even from a distance, Tahirah could hear the sultan grit his teeth.

Maryam, veiled before her brother-in-law, spoke cautiously. "Sire, it's not my place, but out of my love for my sister's memory, I would speak. The child meant no harm. Ara was only trying to aid my daughter. Her curiosity sometimes gets the better of her, but this is a forgivable quality in one so young. Especially one who lost her mother so early. But this, ah, inquisitiveness is offset by her good heart, kindness and the care she shows to those she loves. I ask that you react not in anger but in the wisdom and reason that you have always shown." She stopped, as though wary of saying too much.

Several servants—who were rushing about trying to appear busy—cautiously peered over their shoulders at the sultan and the bevy of women. The sultan sat stone-faced, staring into space. "Zoriah, how speak you?"

46

The woman in question looked torn for a moment, then set her shoulders decisively. "The harem's peace has been disrupted. The child must come to an understanding of her duty."

Rabab joined in with her quavery voice. "But she's a sweet, well-meaning child—if wild, reckless and willful."

Tahirah coughed as she stifled a chuckle, pulling her shawl across her face. *Painting the girl black with her praise.*

Maryam tried once again. "Ara was born in this very building, was she not? She would never do anything to harm the Alhambra. She's just a very bright child, curious about how things work."

"Oh, yes, she even fusses over the lions of the fountain. Remember when we lost her when she was a bit of a thing? Fell asleep under the lions. It looked for all the world as though they were circled around, protecting her," Rabab recalled. "She insisted the lions talked to her. Of course, she was barely old enough to speak."

Tahirah turned her head to the side. *What's that? The child has an affinity with the stone lions? Of course, Ara was born here. Maybe...*

The sultan leaned back and looked over at the Sufi, acknowledging her with a nod before responding to the women. "You have all had your say. You are free to retire to the harem." The chill in the sultan's voice left no room for discussion. "You will be told when I have made a decision." The women exchanged worried glances and started filing out. Fatima looked as if she wanted to speak again, but Zoriah grabbed her arm and pulled her toward the door.

"Zoriah, stay a moment, my wife. I wish a word with you."

At the doorway, Zoriah spoke quickly with Maryam and Rabab before returning to her husband's side.

Tahirah watched the frown lines disappear from his face as he looked intently at his wife and enclosed her hand affectionately in his. The Sufi stood off to the side, unsure whether or not to approach the throne. The warm blush that rose to her cheeks as she gazed at her husband transformed Zoriah's face. *A marriage of the heart as well as the mind*, thought Tahirah with a smile.

The sultan turned to her as if she had spoken, still clasping his wife's hand, his natural warmth and charm returning. "Greetings in the name of Allah, blessed be His name. I hope you were not distressed by the events of yesterday evening. Please do not think that this is our usual way of entertaining." He smiled, the slightest twinkle returning to his eye. "Would that all my problems were as minor as this."

Tahirah decided to act. "Forgive me, *shaykh*, I could not but overhear. If I could be of some small service." She put out her hand as he started to frown. "Please, hear me out—this is a favor that I ask from you. My life has been one of much work and much travel. Children were not a part of that life. Here is a chance for me to form a bond with a child, a valuable and life-broadening experience. You have a daughter on the verge of womanhood whose exuberances are challenging harem life. Consider letting me take her under my wing. I love to teach, and it would please me."

The sultan sighed and shook his head. "I could not impose on your generosity for such a thing. This is a family matter, a matter between my daughter and me."

"As Allah has granted me no children of my own, it would be a gift to me. I also was a child given to mischief. I remember well how difficult and arbitrary rules seemed. The honor would be mine if you allow me to instruct your child. A curious child whose mind is occupied has less time to err. I would consider it a kindness. Perhaps she and her cousin could show me around the palace, and I could engage their energies toward scholarship and learning."

The sultan glanced at Zoriah with a shrug before responding. "Perhaps it would be worth a try. She *is* a smart girl. I would be grateful for whatever interest you show her. I have no wish to inflict pain on my child, but she must learn responsibility and to live in harmony within the harem." He turned to his wife. "Do you agree? Will this solution please the others?"

Zoriah stood still before finally nodding. "Yes, that will do. Also, I can start her training in running a palace."

The sultan smiled and proclaimed, "Done, it is decided. We can work out the details later."

Chapter 12

Ara heard the sound of footsteps at her bedside and felt Layla's anxious presence beyond her closed lids. "Are you awake?" Her quiet voice whispered.

Ara opened her eyes. "Yes, but I want to rest." Her face was still blotchy from crying. "Su'ah spent all morning fussing over me. She kept pouring vile teas into me. She was certain I was going to break out in spots." Ara shifted listlessly. "I want to go back to sleep."

"Are you sure you're not sick? You look awful. This is the second day you've stayed in bed." Layla's voice was soft with worry. "What's wrong? You know I had to tell your father about the dye. He asked me directly. He was angry, but he said no real harm was done."

Ara kept her eyes closed. Harm had been done by her...and nothing would ever be right again.

Layla continued, remorse lacing her voice. "Did Suleiman yell at you about the dye? He went looking for you as soon as he saw it in the fountain. He said I looked guilty, but he knew who was responsible."

"Where is Su—I mean, the lizard?" Ara asked suddenly. "How did you keep Su'ah from finding him?"

A frown crossed Layla's face and she sat down on the bed. "The lizard? He's in my sewing basket. I couldn't think of any other place. No one goes through my embroidery. I offered him bugs, but he didn't move." She made a face, then straightened, looking provoked. "Why are we hiding a lizard?"

Su'ah burst into the room. "Did you hear, Ara? Tahirah has offered to instruct you. Think of that! I'm so pleased for you." She bustled about, grabbing clothes, hairbrushes and a sponge. "Tahirah was quite adamant, I understand, about seeing you immediately. If she gets some horrible disease from you, it won't

50

be my fault. I told her servants that you were under the weather, but no one listens to me."

"I don't want to go anywhere." Ara laid her head back on the pillow. All her hopes and dreams were gone, crushed by one folly. Nothing was important now. She deserved to be in the coldest dungeon, not basking in the light of a Sufi.

"I don't know what's wrong with you, child, but unless you have a fever, you can't mope around the rest of your life. You're getting up right now. No more of this." Su'ah nodded in emphasis. "Why, it's almost afternoon. Now, come here, and let's get you tidied." She pulled back the covers on Ara's bed. "By the way, where is Suleiman? I couldn't find him all yesterday. Just like a man, always underfoot except when you need him. I heard talk that he was on an errand for Tahirah, but no one seems to know where."

Su'ah limped stiffly over to the door and looked up and down the hallway. "He should be the one to walk you over to the mathemagician's rooms. She's in the Palace of the Partal, you know. Even though it's inside the fortress walls, I don't like you wandering around by yourself. There are too many foreigners coming and going. People who aren't used to our ways."

"What?" Ara looked up, suddenly interested. "What did you say about Suleiman?"

"So that's the way of it, is it? I knew something was upsetting you. Did you and Suleiman have a falling-out?"

"No," she said sadly, "we didn't quarrel. I just didn't know about the errand." *Tahirah couldn't have sent Suleiman on an errand.* An image of Suleiman transformed into a lizard flashed before her. "Must I go?"

"I can't believe this. Last week you would have traded me *and* Suleiman to see this woman. Now you can't be bothered? You *are* going, and that is that. Your father is so proud that she's taking an interest in you." Su'ah abruptly turned and slapped the clothes down. "You're fortunate to have been unwell. Time has softened his anger. I don't know what he would have done if

Tahirah hadn't intervened for you. What were you thinking? The dye in the fountain upset the whole harem."

"Tahirah spoke to Father about the dye?" Ara asked, reluctantly sitting up so Su'ah could brush her hair. *Why is Tahirah involved? Is she working with the wazir?*

"She overheard him speaking to Zoriah about you. He was plenty upset with you. You're lucky the Sufi offered to instruct you." Su'ah gave Ara's hair a final swipe with the brush. "Bread and water for the next month was the way I heard it. Tahirah intervened with a different plan, and he agreed."

"What are they going to do to me?"

"You'll hear that from the mathemagician, I would guess," Su'ah said, nodding sagely. She turned Ara around. "Is that it? Have you been listening to gossip about Sufis?"

Alarms went off in Ara's head. *Was the Sufi an evil mathemagician also? But that didn't seem right.* She remembered the voice that had urged her to leave the room of broken mirrors. She'd been told her mother had loved this teacher. Ara debated with herself for a moment before trusting herself to speak.

"I'll go. If Father insists, I'll go," she said grudgingly. "But why only me? Must I go by myself?"

"Actually, Tahirah requested that your cousin join you. Now, let's get you dressed."

Ara looked over at her cousin. Layla looked stricken, and asked nervously, "Am I in trouble too? Are we going to be punished?"

"You need to ask your parents that question. It's not my business, but you know you girls have been traipsing around causing trouble..." Su'ah's words drifted off.

"I didn't do anything. I never would. What must Mother think?" Layla sobbed.

"Child, I'm sure it will be fine." Su'ah patted Layla's back soothingly. "Maybe the Sufi wants to teach you also."

"Noooo. I'm terrible at math. That can't be it at all." Layla's face was turning pink and splotchy.

Soon, four silent servants escorted the girls out of the Palace of the Myrtles, around the Mosque, and through a myriad of enclosed gardens toward the Sufi's rooms. Neither girl spoke. They passed other children on the way; Jada ducked her head as they passed, and Hasan, trailed by his younger brothers, grinned his encouragement. Ara felt numb.

Though it was only a few stones' throw distance, the journey to the Sufi's rooms seemed to take forever.

Ara's mind swirled. *Why does Tahirah wish to see us? I won't let her hurt Layla or Suleiman,* she swore to herself.

Layla glided beside her like a ghost, wearing the haunted look of one condemned. Her embroidery basket was clutched in her hands, and her knuckles were white.

Ara saw little hope for a rosy future. *Suleiman is a lizard, the wazir is evil, and I am powerless to stop him. If only I had not been so curious. No one would ever believe me even if I confessed what happened. And now, even Layla is in trouble because of me.*

Chapter 13

Tahirah contemplated the two tense and unhappy children who stood in her doorway. The leggy filly of a child with the defiant glare must be Ara. If she were a cat, that heavy black braid of hers would be lashing back and forth. The other girl, Layla, stared at the floor. The servants bowed out of the room, promising to return before the next prayer.

"Good afternoon," Tahirah began. "I greet you in the joy of Allah. Blessed be his name."

Layla whispered back, "Blessed be."

Silence.

"Perhaps you should sit down. I thought we might have some tea and get to know each other." How did people speak to the young? She had no idea. This might be harder than expected.

Ara sat down, her back straight as if prepared for battle, with Layla close beside her. These poor girls are obviously terrified. Tahirah picked up the ewer and poured the contents into three cups. She passed the steaming mint tea to each of the children before sitting down on a cushion herself. "Bismillah, 'in the name of God'," I had a tray of baklava brought up. These are made with pistachios and Grenadian honey. I thought you might enjoy some."

In the quiet that followed, Tahirah took a sip of tea. "I hope that we might become friends." The smaller girl looked up hopefully for a second, then focused once more on the floor. Ara was obviously having none of it. Tahirah watched them through lowered lashes. Neither of the girls touched the teacups.

She thought about the previous evening when she had felt evil magic closing in on Ara and had used her power to urge her away. The taint had left Tahirah weak. Sleep had eluded her. She wished her inner vision had been clearer. She needed this girl to confide in her, but how could she gain her trust? Here was a challenge almost as difficult as unraveling a theorem. She took a deep breath and concentrated on the problem. Her magic was of learning. This was just another mathematics problem. Though, she thought with a sigh, perhaps as tangled as one could be.

"Why did you have us brought here?" Ara finally demanded, her arm wrapped protectively around her cousin's shoulder.

"To have tea and baklava with me. Is that so unreasonable?" Tahirah replied, confused by the girl's anger.

Ara looked around the room. There were no mirrors, broken or not. She couldn't figure out if the mathemagician was good or evil. She sneaked a look at her—and was startled by the warmth of violet eyes. Was Tahirah the one who had warned her away in the mirrored room? She glanced at the mathemagician, who sat as if waiting for her answer. Well, thought Ara, she is going to wait for a long time.

She frowned and stared at the wall behind Tahirah. Another vertical reflection symmetry—that would be the third. But no, it wasn't right; one tile in the band was twisted, so it wasn't a perfect reflection. As she watched, the tile wiggled and turned before her startled eyes. Now it matched the rest. *What was that?* She stared again, not sure that she had truly seen it move.

A noise came from Layla's embroidery basket, then right after, another noise far away, almost like a roar. The basket bounced. Layla dropped it and backed away. Ara grabbed it, hugging it to herself protectively. Tahirah looked at it in surprise.

"Arrrrrrr...Arrrrrrra..." came from the basket.

Its lid thumped up and down. They all stared. "What have you done, child?" Tahirah asked Ara.

"I...I can't tell you," she stammered. The racket from the basket was getting louder.

"As Allah is good, I think you truly must tell me. Daughter of the harem, something is very wrong here," exclaimed Tahirah.

Something is very wrong indeed, she thought to herself as she watched the basket's lid open and a green snake, twice as long as Layla's arm and half as thick as her wrist, slithered out. Layla backed up against the wall and covered her eyes with her hands.

"Oh, no," cried Ara. "Where's Suleiman? Please, as Allah is merciful, let him not have been eaten by a snake." Ara riffled madly through the basket. Embroidery scattered everywhere.

The snake raised its head and spoke. "Arrrrra, I promissssed."

"A transformation," whispered Tahirah in a shocked voice and watched the snake wind its way across the floor. "Is that Suleiman?"

"No, Suleiman is a lizard," Ara wailed. "Not a snake. He must have been eaten."

"I think not," Tahirah said carefully. "Truly, that is your servant, before us in snake form. And he calls you. Tell me, what did Suleiman promise?"

"Nothing," Ara said, sniffling. Then she remembered. "Well, just a silly thing about mathemathics. But what happened to the lizard? Why did he change?" She saw her cousin shrinking into the wall. "Layla's afraid of snakes."

Layla, pressed up against the wall, peered out from between her fingers.

Reaching out her hand, Tahirah said, "I think we are all going to have to be very brave here, Layla. Come and sit next to me. Suleiman has been bespelled, and this is going to take all our efforts to resolve."

"I can't." Layla leaned farther away.

"Yes, you can. I'll help you be brave. Don't think of him as a snake, but as your friend, Suleiman, who's in trouble and needs your help." Tahirah's voice enveloped the girl like a protective hijab.

Layla, still eyeing the snake, slowly scooted forward to sit at Tahirah's side, and Tahirah turned to Ara. "Now, I want you to tell

56

me everything you know about how this happened. I particularly want to know about this promise."

Hesitantly at first, Ara told the story of the wazir. She told about the frogs, the broken mirrors, the tiles changing, and finally about Suleiman turning into a lizard. Tahirah listened gravely with Layla tucked into her arm. The snake had wrapped itself around Ara's wrist like a bracelet and lay quietly there.

"I see. This explains much. Did Suleiman speak to you before, in his lizard shape?"

The girls looked at one another. "No, he just lay curled in a ball," Ara responded finally.

"And the promise," Tahirah asked. "How did that come to be?"

"He was teaching me band symmetry, and I made him promise to teach me more. I remember he swore on his tribe's honor," she said excitedly. "Would that mean something?"

Tahirah sat and thought. She looked at the snake, and then at Ara. "What exactly was the promise?"

"He promised to teach me all seven band symmetries. He had just taught me vertical reflection symmetry and sent me to find three examples before he would teach me the others. But he promised he would once I found three examples. And they had to be correct. Just now I saw that last one over there, but it wasn't right, it was twisted," she said pointing, "and then it changed and fixed itself." She looked to see if Tahirah believed her, but the mathemagician's face gave nothing away.

"And then I asked him about the tile that I saw change and he said it wasn't possible. That if a tile could change, so could he— Oh, did that have something to do with him becoming a snake? The symmetry fixing itself?"

They all turned to look at the symmetry. It was a reflection. The gold shapes flipped over and over across the wall.

57

"See, each one is the mirror of the one before and they flip over a vertical line," Ara said. "After it changed, the thumping began."

"It repaired itself, or did you repair it? The Alhambra must listen to you indeed." Tahirah was quiet as she stared at the wall. The tile was now smooth and flat.

"How long ago did Suleiman make you this promise?" the Sufi asked.

"It was about two days after you arrived. Suleiman was angry with me for being outside the palace to watch the parade." Ara stopped, aghast at her unplanned confession.

"Yes, I felt you that day." Tahirah closed her eyes. "Your aura radiated excitement, fear and joy. Such a strong presence you are, child. I remember being curious about a girl so daring and bold. Much like me when I was your age," she said with a slow smile. "Now, let's see, let me check my journal for the exact date." Pausing, she rose and walked over to a little niche in her room. She picked up a small book and quickly flipped through its pages. "Yes, as I thought. I arrived three weeks ago today, so Suleiman was bound by his promise exactly twenty-one days ago. How interesting," she murmured, calculating numbers in her head. "There are seven band symmetries, and Suleiman asked you to find three examples of the first symmetry." She glanced at the girls. The snake around Ara's arm was turning in agitated circles.

"Promisssssed, Arrrrra. You helpppp," Suleiman hissed, looking at Tahirah.

"Hmm. We have a two-fold problem," she said finally. "Suleiman made you a promise three weeks ago. You found two examples of vertical symmetry, but this third one was broken, tainted by the magic of the wazir. When you saw it and noted its wrongness, it was able to heal itself. Then Suleiman also changed from a lizard into a snake.

"This is helpful. The bands of magic holding him are more fragile then the wazir thinks. It is also hopeful that Suleiman now speaks. He remembers being human and is fighting off the spells." She looked off and gathered her thoughts.

"We need to continue your education in symmetries," she said, nodding her head emphatically. "Because of his promise to teach you each of the band symmetries, I believe we may have a way to restore Suleiman. The wazir's magic was incompletely drawn. A promise, especially one coupled with tribal honor, is binding." She stopped suddenly, and considered.

"The wazir tied his evil magic to Suleiman. That may yet be his undoing." She looked intensely at Ara. "As the palace heals, so does Suleiman. You are the catalyst: the daughter of the Alhambra born of the line of the Nazrids. The Alhambra was betrayed by one of its own, the wazir, and it is distrustful.

"You must continue finding the symmetries. You need to seek out the damaged tiles for each symmetry. This reminds the Alhambra of its strength. It fights the spell, just as Suleiman does. If we are particularly fortunate, releasing Suleiman from this binding should also undo the evil the wazir has twisted into the Alhambra. Though whether Suleiman or the Alhambra will fully heal, I cannot say."

Ara sat unmoving, struck by the enormity of the task placed before her, and laid a protective hand on Suleiman.

Tahirah was silent for some minutes before speaking. "Well, we must do what we can. Magic, as you know, is as logical and ordered as mathematics. To reverse this spell, time is halved and then halved again."

She looked up at the two silent children, their eyes wide in worry—and yet a touch of hope flickered there. "The Alhambra's magic is at risk. If this evil continues, the Alhambra will fall."

Layla turned even whiter; Ara looked down to hide her fear and, seeing the snake on her arm, nodded, remembering.

"Father has been really worried this spring, but he said that the Alhambra protects its own. Is the symmetry magic how it's done?"

Tahirah smiled encouragingly at Ara. "It's more complicated than that, but yes, magic is buried in the symmetries, and Suleiman is now tied to that magic.

"And now, we are working against time. If it took you twenty-one days from the time of Suleiman's promise till you found the symmetries, you have only half that time to find the next and half again for the one after." Tahirah looked very grave. "We are in a race to save both Suleiman and the Alhambra. If we can pull Suleiman out of this enchantment, some of the wazir's evil may be broken and the Alhambra's strength regained."

"I see," said Layla, perking up. "Because Ara completed the first task set by Suleiman in twenty-one days, then the next task needs to be found in ten and one-half days, then five and one-quarter days." She looked worried. "I guess you have to figure hours after that." She wrinkled her nose.

"Yes, sixty-three hours, thirty-one and one-half hours, fifteen hours and forty-five minutes. Each time it halves. That will mean the last symmetry must be found in under eight hours." Tahirah looked up gravely. "We are lucky it took you so long to find all the examples of the first symmetry. A shorter time would be almost impossible for us." She stopped for a moment, lost in thought as she gazed out her latticed window.

The responsibility dizzied Ara. "But it's still not enough time. I could never find them all. I don't even know the other symmetry patterns. How can I find broken ones if I don't even know what the correct ones look like?"

"Well, as it happens, I know those symmetries," Tahirah said with a quiet smile. "If Suleiman will wrap himself around my wrist, I can act as his...assistant. We can do this." She looked at Layla. "And you will help as well, won't you?"

"I can't. I'm not good at geometry like Ara, and I'm not brave and..."

Tahirah squeezed Layla's shoulder reassuringly. "You are. Everyone can do mathematics. It may be easier for some, but everyone can master the principles. We need you. Suleiman is counting on us. Both mathematics and bravery can be learned. You must decide if it's important to you. Suleiman needs all of us now."

Layla ducked her head. "But it's so very hard for me."

"It's going to be hard for all of us," Tahirah said. "Hard for Ara to keep her counsel about Suleiman and not to accidentally betray herself before the wazir. Hard for me to admit I need the help of two girls to solve a mathemagical problem—and very hard for Suleiman to be a snake. He has placed his faith in us, and we hold the key to his release. We can lean on each other for strength. I'll help you learn symmetry. Ara and you will help me learn about teaching girls. Oath?" she held out her hand.

"Oath," both girls replied, their voices solemn, and grasped her hand in a three-way clasp.

Chapter 14

"But why did you bring us here in the first place?" Ara asked, turning her head to the side. "We thought we were being punished."

Astonishment and hurt flashed in Tahirah's eyes. "Do you think me an evil djinn? I hoped you would prefer me to the diet of bread and water that had been suggested."

Ara mouthed the word, "Oh."

"I thought we could explore the Alhambra together. I would teach you mathematics and Sufi mysticism."

Tahirah tilted her head up at the ceiling's honeycombed recesses and winced. "The Alhambra is in pain—I can feel it—I had a vision showing a key. I believe both of you are part of that key."

Ara reached one hand out, touching the ceramic tiled wall as if to comfort the Alhambra.

"My visions are sometimes cloudy, but this one was crystal clear. I spoke with Suleiman only hours before he was transformed. He offered to go into town for me to retrieve a scroll. He spoke with such pride about the two of you." A sudden memory made her shake her head. "I do think that you should begin by removing the red stains from the lions' chests. The color makes them restless, hungering for a kill. They are lions, after all. Your father wished them cleaned, and I agreed to see that it was done," she added. "I hope you don't mind."

"The stone lions? They have feelings?" Layla asked.

"Of course they do, though they are lions, and their thoughts are not like yours and mine. They were created long ago as defenders of the Palace of Lions, placed in its central court facing out in twelve directions, so that none could approach without their knowledge. Each lion was imbued with a trait to support the sultan."

"Do you talk to them?" asked Ara.

"I have tried." she replied directly to Ara. "But they have not responded. Nor is your father's lion at his side. I worry...perhaps it's just that they don't trust easily or perhaps many things. We can't know."

"My father has his own lion?"

Tahirah looked thoughtful. "Yes, it is said each lion trails the ruler of the Alhambra, though not every ruler of the Alhambra is granted the ability to see this wonder."

"But if you can see them, why won't they talk to you?" Ara asked.

"They are the guardians of the castle and are wary of outside magic." Tahirah responded candidly. "I'm still not sure what the wazir is trying to do. Why is he harming the Alhambra?" she mused, then shook her slender shoulders. "Is he embroiled with the Castilians or with the Saracens or the Aragons—or some other group entirely—or is he on his own?" She closed her eyes. "All in good time, as Allah wills. We have more pressing business. I need to teach you the next symmetry. Here, Suleiman, come and wrap around my wrist so we can do this together," she spoke directly to the snake, extending her arm.

Suleiman uncoiled himself from Ara's wrist and slithered across the floor to Tahirah. "Let's see, Suleiman taught you mirror symmetry across a vertical line, right?" she asked. The snake rested unblinking in his new location. "My thought is that the second one learned should be mirror symmetry over a horizontal line. We should probably review both." She pulled out a quill and paper and launched into her lecture.

"You remember that symmetry is a relationship of characteristic correspondence, equivalence, or identity among constituents of a system. In mathematics it is a property that generates repeated patterns. Band symmetry, which we are focusing on here, runs in one direction like a frieze or border. Euclid stated in his treatise that there is a connection between—"

63

"Actually no, I don't remember what you're saying at all," Ara interrupted, startled by the complicated words. Layla sat beside her, looking despondent.

"No?" Tahirah asked, surprised. "That's the way my instructor presented it to me. How did Suleiman explain it to you?"

"Well, a lot simpler. He did talk about repeated patterns though," Ara answered uncomfortably.

Suleiman raised his head, "Ssssymtry is sssimple."

"I see. Let's start over, shall we?" Tahirah took a deep breath and tried to recall herself as a young girl. "I've got it. Symmetry is about two things, pattern and motion—in particular, which motions a pattern can make and still remain the same.

"Let's draw some simple patterns. Ara, you draw one, and Layla, you can draw the next. I'm going to explain reflection or mirror symmetry across a horizontal line."

"Suleiman called it a flip," Ara interjected.

"He did, did he?" Tahirah frowned at the snake in her lap. "All right then, reflection, mirror or flip—all three are names of this motion. Each of you draw something simple on the parchment. Just one thing each!"

She smiled at them. "Lovely. Those are excellent. Now we

shall pretend there is a line below them that they reflect...oh, sorry, flip over. Watch. I will draw the horizontal mirror image, or flip, of each of your images. The horizon is an imaginary line that stretches left to right across a landscape," she added by way of explanation. "See how these images are now 'flipped' across the imaginary line below them. A perfect match, if we were to see it in a mirror." Tahirah hesitated as she looked at each girl. Ara's eyes were bright with comprehension as she focused on the drawing. The dawning of understanding crept more slowly across Layla's face.

"But what about the line? How can you find an imaginary line?" the girl asked.

"Good question, Layla," Tahirah said, then considered. "Well, you are looking for a place where the pattern would be repeated. In the drawings you just did, we placed the line beneath the first pattern. That was the easy way, starting with an object, drawing a line under it or beside it and completing the symmetry yourself. But how do you find the symmetry in an already completed object?" She looked at both girls. "Any guesses?"

"Maybe you could cover a pattern until only half of it shows?" asked Ara.

"Yes," Tahirah agreed. "And there are other ways. Think about mirrors."

"You could hold a mirror up to it and see if the other half of the pattern is repeated," Layla offered.

"Good. Now, let's continue. The vertical flip goes left or right, correct?" Tahirah ran her hand across the contented snake. "That's what you learned from Suleiman and the kind of symmetry you were searching for. In the horizontal flip, the pretend line goes across, and the pattern flips up or down. Let's practice the symmetry in repeated patterns. Here, I will draw a few and you tell me if they are horizontally symmetric or not." She reached for her quill and ink. "This is a test," she said, smiling. "Here I will present a whole row of the symmetry as you would see it in the tiling of the Alhambra."

"That's easy," said Layla. "It's a horizontal symmetry."

"Excellent. And this one," Tahirah said, sketching madly.

"There," Ara exclaimed, reaching over to trace an imaginary line with her finger. "The middle of the budlike thing. If you divide it in half, the whole pattern is flipped over."

"Good. And here is yet another."

66

The girls looked at one another. Ara stated, "Well, I see a

line that splits it in half exactly, but if you flip it over, it doesn't match up. The triangles on the top would land in the blank space."

"Perfect." Tahirah smiled. "This is *not* horizontal mirror symmetry, just as you said. It does have symmetry, but not the ones we are speaking of today. How about this?"

"Oh, I see it," Layla said, pleased. "That's what Ara showed me. It's a vertical flip. I remember she said that the line runs from the earth all the way to Allah. I see that there would be a line between the heads of the chickens going up and down." The snake had lifted his head during the discussion and seemed pleased also.

Tahirah reached over and squeezed Layla's shoulder. "I am

very impressed. That was excellent. There is one further requirement for the images you search for. It must have a horizontal symmetry, but it cannot also have a vertical symmetry."

"What?" Ara looked up. "How could it have both?"

"It is possible for both horizontal and vertical symmetry to exist in one design. But for our purposes you must eliminate any designs that you find with both, as they will not break the spell. The only symmetry it can have is a horizontal reflection. Can you remember this?"

"Yes," the girls agreed, though they both were somewhat surprised by this new requirement.

Tahirah glanced outside at the sky and looked worried. "We have only one and one-half weeks for the two of you to find the horizontal symmetry damaged by the wazir's magic. But first, the stone lions must be washed clean of the red dye. Of most immediate importance, we need to protect Suleiman in his snake form. I will do some mathematical searching to find out why the wazir is destroying the magic in the palace." She stopped, suddenly aware of afternoon shadows. "It is getting late. We must end this lesson. Such a short time to resolve a difficult spell." Concern in her eyes, Tahirah looked down at the snake.

"How do I know where the wazir broke it? It could be anywhere in the Palace of the Lions or the Palace of the Myrtles, even in the Palace of the Partal..." asked Ara. The importance of her task overwhelmed her.

"We can't know. He is putting pressure somewhere, but the magic ripples throughout the Alhambra, finding a weak spot. There it breaks a symmetry. It could appear anywhere.

"You must not attract the attention of the wazir. If too many people know that you search for symmetries, broken symmetries, he also will know. But Layla can help, can't you?"

"I think so." She looked at the green snake wrapped around Tahirah's wrist and shuddered. "Will I have to touch the slimy snake?"

"Yes, in fact, you need to hold him now. Layla, your life has been sheltered in the palace, but one who loves and cares for you is in trouble. His life is in your hands. Remember, this is Suleiman, and he's having a very difficult time." Gently, she placed Suleiman in Layla's lap.

The snake curled into a relaxed S-curve. He picked his head up and stared at Layla. "Nottt ssslimy. Llayylla ccowarddd!" he hissed, bobbing his head up and down.

"I am not," she exclaimed. "Well, maybe I am timid, a bit, but it is unkind of you to say so." Then she grinned and laughed. "I'm talking to a snake!" She reached out her hand to pet him. "Why, he's soft like satin. I never knew. Oh, Suleiman, I'm so, so sorry. I'll help you, I promise."

"Nottt cccowardd. Bbrave and kkind," Suleiman responded with a satisfied flick of his tongue.

Chapter 15

"Beet juice isn't easy to get off," Ara complained, scrubbing the lion with big bristled brushes. She felt a tremor beneath her hand. She crouched down and stared into the lion's eyes, her fingers cupping his chin. "Hello. Can you hear me?"

Nothing changed. She sighed loudly and continued washing down the lion. "How many of them are done?"

"This is the third lion," her cousin answered. "There are nine more." Layla paused, pushing her braids out of her face. "How is Suleiman? I worried about him all last night."

"Fine," Ara replied, checking under her caftan for the snake that wrapped around her waist. "He's still asleep. He was really cranky when we put him back in your basket last night. He was hissing so much, I was afraid Su'ah would hear him. When I woke him at dawn, he was so annoyed he threatened to bite me. He was nicer as a lizard," she added with some emphasis.

"I think he was too upset before to be anything but sad. Now, he's starting to be more himself. Maybe he didn't sleep well last night," Layla offered. "I'd worry too if I had turned into a snake."

"You would be upset because you couldn't dance. I think he's just crabby like always."

"Innssssolent girl-cccchild," hissed a muffled voice.

"Suleiman, you're awake!"

"Yessss." The snake slithered out onto the stone floor and blinked in the bright morning light, then coiled himself, loop upon loop, until he looked much like a bright green rope abandoned on the warm floor. He lifted his head slightly, testing the air with his tongue. "Sssmells quiet."

"Truly?" Layla asked. "Does quiet have a smell? Can you taste it with your tongue?" Now that she had a tentative peace with the snake, she found much about him interesting.

69

"Yesss." He swung his head from side to side, watching them wash the big cats. "Sssmells niccce."

"Suleiman, I don't think you should be there." Ara said nervously. "Someone might come in and see you. What if the wazir should walk by?"

"Sssunshhine. Needd ssunshhine," the snake murmured, slithering off into some small bushes where he could drift back to sleep.

"But Ara, the wazir thinks Suleiman is a lizard," Layla stated as she rubbed a stain from the chin of a lion. "So we don't have to worry, do we?"

"We need to be careful. He's a very evil man," Ara whispered, remembering Suleiman's cry for mercy in the mirrored room. "And you heard Tahirah tell us to stay far away from him. If he discovers that Suleiman has been transformed, he will be suspicious. We must find all the symmetries and turn Suleiman back to normal before he notices." They continued scouring the narrow nooks and crevices in the marble manes and toes.

"Besides," Ara continued, "snakes never get into the palace. There are people who would be afraid and might hurt him. Remember how you felt? Your mother would faint."

Despite her concern for Suleiman, Layla grinned at the thought of her mother's reaction to a snake. Then she said, "I was afraid because I didn't understand how nice they are. They eat rats and mice and are very quiet. Mother thinks they are slimy—and you know they aren't."

"I don't think now is a good time for her to find that out." Ara checked the arched doorways once again. "It's important that we keep this secret. Tahirah said that as long as people thought Suleiman was on an errand for her, they might as well keep thinking so. Aside from us, no one but the wazir knows what really happened to him."

Her uneasiness deepened, and her hands felt raw from scrubbing. "How are we ever going to find all the symmetries in time? We can't ask many people for help or the wazir might find out." They both pondered this a moment. "Well, we have access to the whole palace, and that should be enough. Tahirah can't come with us or the wazir would be on to us for certain. She is a mathemagician, after all."

Layla looked up from her work, frowning. "Does the wazir know that she's tutoring us?"

"Who would tell him? The harem's business is not his concern. Father would not think to talk to him about the doings of the women and children of the harem."

"Do you really think Suleiman will turn back into a person?" Layla lowered her voice and looked around nervously. "It all seems so strange and scary. At least he speaks a bit."

"Tahirah thinks he will continue to heal as the symmetry magic heals the Alhambra. So it must be true," Ara responded.

"I still don't understand why we don't tell your father. He could just arrest the wazir and put him in the dungeon. Then everyone would be safe," her cousin said, going back to a previous argument.

"Layla, Father still won't even talk to me. He had his manservant give Su'ah the brushes and soap and tell her that he didn't want to see me until all the lions were sparkling clean. Maybe not even then." She lowered her voice to a whisper. "What if the wazir turned my father into a frog before he was locked up? We need proof. And not just a snake who looks nothing like Suleiman."

"I don't know about that," Layla said, peeking over the bushes at the sleeping snake. "There's something about his eyes and the way his head shakes."

Ara threw a soap-laden rag at her, and they chased each other laughingly around the fountain. Finally, they stood leaning over the fountain, giggling and catching their breath.

"Do you think Tahirah is right about the stone lions? You know, that they have feelings?"

"It could be. When I was very little, I believed my stone lion loved and protected me." She looked up at Layla's questioning eyes and made an embarrassed shrug. "I was very young! It could be true. Tahirah said they are wary of outside magic, but you and I don't have any magic, and they have known us, well, *forever*. Do you think they might talk to people without magic?" She looked hopefully over her shoulder at her favorite. "*Maybe* he will talk to me. Anyway, let's save him for last so we can give him a particularly good scrub."

The crunch of many footsteps came upon them before they could react. Zoriah and Fatima came in wrapped in their hijabs, followed by a pair of harem guards in liveried dress. Alarmed, Ara glanced at the bushes but could not see Suleiman. Layla scrubbed at the lion more vigorously.

Zoriah looked critically at the girls. "I see Layla is working hard. Ara, you're taking a bit of a break? Tahirah was called away to Lindejarras early this morning and asked me to come and tell you. She had hoped to oversee your education while she is here, but that will have to be put off for a day or so."

Ara's face fell.

"I see this is a disappointment to you, but there it is. Your father asked me to help in her and Suleiman's absence." She furrowed her brow and spoke to Fatima. "Do you know when is he due back? He's been too long away from the Alhambra."

Fatima shrugged, as if unwilling to acknowledge her lack of gossip on the subject.

Zoriah turned back to Ara and Layla. "I'm glad that you are making some progress cleaning this up. A delegation from the North arrives next week, and your father will receive them in the Hall of the Kings. Refreshments will be served in here. This room must be spotless. I am sure that you girls will see that it is so." But her voice didn't sound sure to Ara.

Fatima glowered at Ara in disapproval. "I would like to say that I'm astonished at your behavior, but I'm not. You break rules like twigs, and no one but me seems to be concerned. I was prostrate with fright when I saw blood in the fountain. It's not for me to say, but I don't understand why your father lets you get away with so much."

Zoriah touched her arm as if to contain her, but Fatima shrugged her off, saying, "And Layla, I *am* surprised that you were involved. You were a nice child, but I see you've been led astray." She sniffed. "I don't know how many times I've told your mother what a bad influence Ara is. She defends you both, but I see that I was right."

"Fatima, Mother of my Mother, remember that it was just beet juice," Zoriah said calmly. "I think we should let the girls go back to their task, don't you? I'm sure they are very sorry that you were upset."

"Of course, they are sorry now. But the wazir agrees with me. It was an omen, blood or whatever. He told me so. An omen of death and destruction."

"Fatima! We have business elsewhere," Zoriah interrupted in a determined voice. She moved to the door and out of the room, gently pushing Fatima before her.

The girls were quiet for a moment after the women's departure. "But she promised to help us," Layla frowned, thinking of Tahirah.

Ara almost wept in frustration. "What could be so important that she would leave us now?" And what would she do without Tahirah? Then another thought hit her. What would she do without Layla?

"Does your mother really think I'm a bad influence on you? Would she separate us?"

"Mother thinks that Fatima is old-fashioned and oversteps her authority. Didn't she look just like an angry crow in her black hijab?" Layla said, a bit shocked at her own outburst. "Mother won't keep us apart. She says you're full of life and have a good heart. She told me you remind her of your mother when she was a girl."

"Really?" Ara asked with relief, bouncing back to her normal confidence. "Well, I think Fatima looks like a *well-fed* angry crow," she whispered, giggling. "Tahirah will be back, I'm sure of it. We just need to find the broken symmetries as fast as we can so Suleiman can change."

"Where should we look first?"

"Well, I thought we might—did you see that?" Ara stared at the fountain. "I thought I saw one of my lion's ears flicker."

"It must have been the stone catching the light," Layla said, stepping up to the lion.

Ara shrugged. "You're probably right. I'm just being wishful."

The call to prayer rang out, signaling the end of their chore.

"Done with scrubbing for the rest of the day," Ara said, sagging against her favorite lion.

"I thought it would never be noon. I can't believe we have to do this for a whole week," Layla said wearily. She shook her head. It had been a long morning.

Ara woke Suleiman, ignoring his complaints, and carefully hid the snake in the folds of her clothes. Behind them an ear flicked in their direction and then turned back to stone, frozen beneath the sunlight.

Chapter 16

"Have you found it?" Layla whispered to Ara.

The harem was assembled for the afternoon meal around the Court of the Myrtles. Suleiman had been left sound asleep in Layla's embroidery basket. The low hum of chattering women and children filled the room.

"No, Zoriah is making sure I'm busy every day. She thinks I have too much time on my hands. She says, 'Allah hates idle hands.' Fatima must be talking to her. Have you had any luck?" she asked.

"No. There may be a horizontal symmetry in the Hall of the Two Sisters. Mother and Father walked through there last night on the way to the garden, and I got to go with them. I thought I saw it on the north wall as we were passing through. I didn't get close enough to see if it was broken or not." A small child toddled by and scrambled up into Layla's lap. She kissed his cheek, and the toddler snuggled up against her, thumb in mouth. His mother, Dananir, looked over to make sure her son was content before continuing her conversation with Jada.

Ara grinned at the babe and then looked around the court to make certain no one was listening to them. "As soon as the meal is over, let's go over to the Hall. The days are passing too quickly."

Layla wrinkled her nose in distress. "Couldn't we go later this afternoon? I have dance lessons next."

"I'm supposed to sit with Rabab and sew. Zoriah saw my stitching and said schooling in the womanly arts were in order." Ara rolled her eyes. "I can't wait until Tahirah gets back and we continue our lessons. We have to find those symmetries soon."

"I know," Layla agreed, thinking hard. "What if I join you this afternoon for your sewing lesson. Where are you going to meet Rabab?"

"Beside the fountain where the fig tree is," Ara said, pointing out the window.

"Dance practice is not too long. I'll be there as soon as I finish."

Zoriah stood up and clapped her hands once sharply to get the group's attention. "The representatives from our northern neighbors are coming this Saturday—some will bring their wives. Maryam, I want you and Rabab to be in charge of the food."

She turned toward Rabab, who was whispering in Fatima's ear. "The Spanish women from Castile and Aragon cover their faces as we do. But I am told that the French women cover neither their hair nor faces. Rabab, you need to inform the servants so they do not stare."

"The Infidels are bringing unveiled women?" Fatima cried, aghast.

"Their ways are different from ours. We also will not stare. You must remember that the *shaykh*, our sultan, is working to prevent Granada from becoming embroiled in the conflicts of the North. He will be negotiating tribute agreements with the Northern kings." Zoriah finished smoothly.

Her words produced a buzzing among the women. Finally, Dananir spoke up. "Of course, we wish to help the *shaykh* in this, but we are unused to the People of the Book. How can we go to this meeting? The Christian women know not our ways, and we know not theirs."

Zoriah spoke with the authority of an experienced leader. "The sultan trusts each of us to behave modestly and courteously, as befits a woman. Layla will dance for the women and children. Ara, you will accompany her. You need to be on hand, as you are gifted with languages." Her smile challenged anyone to make more objections. "Everyone must help to make all go smoothly."

The hair prickled on Ara's arm. Did their coming have something to do with the wazir's evil? And even if it didn't, this would make it harder for her to continue her search.

The women drifted out of the room in twos and threes, small children clinging to their mothers or marching stalwartly beside them. Rabab caught Ara's eye and reminded her to collect her sewing supplies before joining her outside.

Ara raced back to her sleeping quarters, checking walls as she ran. She'd never find it in time now. Where was a broken horizontal symmetry?

But the first thing she saw when she entered the room was Layla's sewing basket with its top flung open. Someone had found Suleiman! A sharp hiss caught her attention. There on the cushion curled Suleiman, coiled in a figure eight, his head held high.

"No caggge!" he hissed. "Nott pettt."

"But you can't be loose; people come and go all the time in here. Someone will see you," Ara tried.

"Nnoo cagge!" Suleiman insisted, thrashing when she went to pick him up.

"Suleiman, it's only for a little while. We're trying to undo the magic, really we are. We have over a week to find horizontal symmetries. Please get in the basket. Layla will come soon and take you out, but you need to stay here a little longer. Please, Suleiman!"

She carrying the angry snake across the room and stuffed him unceremoniously into the basket, closing the lid just as Su'ah came in. "Did I hear you call Suleiman's name?" the woman asked. "Is he back from his errand? All the work that needs to be done around here, and he's gallivanting around. I don't know why the sultan let him go." She pressed her lips together in disapproval. "Of course, it's not for me to say."

"Uh, no. I was just thinking aloud that I missed him." Ara held the lid firmly closed. "I have to go to meet Rabab now. Would you tell Layla that I have her basket, please?"

"Of course, child. Here is the sewing you did yesterday. Seems to me a lost cause, but maybe Rabab can succeed where I couldn't. How Zoriah and Rabab hope to train you to be a proper woman, I'd like to know," she said, looking at the stitching with a reproachful eye.

Ara grabbed Layla's basket and hurriedly stuffed her own sewing in a bundle before scooting out of the room. Outside, the sun was warm and a gentle wind blew. Four giggling children ran past her chasing a butterfly. The spring air smelled of jasmine and orange blossoms.

In spite of all this, she was upset at the dilemma she faced. Since his transformation from a lizard into a snake, Suleiman had become less docile. Perhaps that was because he was a snake, or perhaps it was because he was Suleiman—Ara didn't know. It was unimportant why; she still had to keep him hidden and safe. For the hundredth time, she wished Tahirah back at the palace. Rabab's voice carried as she neared the little garden.

"They are dangerous, I tell you. You heard about the French and their Crusades. They took Jerusalem for their own a couple of hundred years ago. Can you imagine *our* holy city in the hands of Infidels? Why, most of them can't even read, and I heard they don't bathe. They even eat snails!"

Ara covered her mouth and giggled, imagining people actually eating the snails that oozed through their gardens.

"But the other countries north of here, Aragon, Castile and Navarre, are worse," Rabab continued. "How could Allah let such ruffians loose in the world? The Toledo library north of here was burned to the ground by those oafs. Centuries of learning burned to ashes in one large bonfire. What kind of people would do that?" Not waiting for a response, she added. "And they're coming *here*. Allah protect us. I'm hiding the silver and the books."

Rounding the corner, Ara saw Rabab and Fatima sitting with their heads together discussing the upcoming meeting.

"Well, as senior member of the harem, I was surprised that the sultan chose Zoriah to organize this event, young as she is. He didn't ask me to attend, not that I would have, you understand. I myself will pray to Allah the whole two days that we aren't murdered in our sleep while they are here," Fatima said.

Rabab vigorously nodded her head in agreement. "There you are, child," she said when Ara entered the garden. Catching her foot on a tree root, Ara pitched forward onto the ground. Rabab shook her head in disbelief. "The dance lessons didn't help, did they?"

Ara peeked under the basket lid, and heaved a sigh of relief that Suleiman was not harmed.

Fatima glowered at the fallen girl protectively clutching her basket and stood up to leave. "Well, I can't dally anymore. Zoriah has taken on a heavy load. She needs me, the daughter of my daughter, whether she will admit it or not. I'm not one to shirk my duty, you know.

"Don't you go embarrassing us," she said, turning to Ara, who was picking herself up. "And just because you can speak Castilian and French, don't go getting above yourself, young lady. Arabic was good enough for Mohammad, blessed be his name, and it's good enough for me." She pursed her lips in disgust. "Allah loves a humble heart. Now brush the dirt off your knees, you're a mess."

"Yes, Fatima. Allah be with you," Ara replied, bowing carefully.

Chapter 17

Ara hadn't been invited to attend the procession. It was just as well, she thought. She needed some time alone to think. The activity in the palace was almost frenzied. Everyone was busy, rushing about to prepare for the visitors. She and Layla had finally finished scrubbing the Lion Fountain two days past. No more red dye could be seen and the floor was as clean as two girls, twelve servants and a lot of lemon juice could make it. Ara had checked her lion once again, laying her hand on his mane and whispering her fears in his ear. There had been no response, just a girl's hopeful imagination.

The previous night, right after she and Layla finished a board game with three of the concubines' sons, the girls made a quick trip to the Hall of the Two Sisters and, after searching three walls, they found a horizontal symmetry in gold and red and blue. But it was perfect, not marred by the wazir's magic.

Even so, Suleiman seemed pleased in his snakelike way and was less difficult that night and all the next morning. Ara looked longingly out of the window one last time before leaving to begin the final preparations. Though, she considered, everything that could be polished, waxed, shined or bathed had been, and thoroughly. Su'ah had sewn a new outfit for her, muttering that no child in her care would look less than regal.

"Ara, there you are. What are you doing up here?" Su'ah said, breathing heavily as she climbed the staircase. "There's work to do. You need to get ready. I have your clothes all laid out."

"Sorry, Su'ah. I wanted a glimpse of the procession." Ara reluctantly turned from the window.

"Guess who is asking for you?" Su'ah said as she crossed the room. "The wazir."

Ara stopped breathing.

"He was worried about you. I mentioned to one of the guards how upset you were the day Suleiman left. Abd al-Rahmid was there. I had him all wrong. I always thought him a selfish, arrogant man, but he seemed truly interested. I told him I would find you so he could speak with you himself.

"It's good that your father has someone that he can trust. These are hard times, and the wazir is a hard man. He was so, even as a boy, but clever and never forgets a detail." Su'ah looked out the window before continuing.

"He, too, is concerned about Suleiman's whereabouts. Actually, I'm worried myself, exasperating as he is. What errand could be taking this long? Ara, are you listening to me or are you daydreaming again?"

Ara jerked herself out of her panic. "Yes, I'm listening. Is Tahirah back yet? Do you know?"

"I heard she is expected back today. Don't know if that's true or not. The house slaves were preparing her rooms this morning. But you know how it is. Sufis move at no one's will but Allah's." She shook her head. "Eager to get out of your sewing lessons, are you? Seems to me time spent learning to wield a needle is of better use than any algebra or geometry or whatever," she rambled on. "Well, hurry up. It isn't polite to keep people waiting. The wazir's a very busy man. He is meeting us in the Court of the Lions. Zoriah and Maryam went to collect Layla."

Ara spun around. "He's going to talk with Layla!"

"Stop dawdling, child, there is much to do. The wazir only wants to ask if either of you've heard from Suleiman. It's nothing for you to be troubled about," she said impatiently.

Ara felt butterflies the size of birds in her stomach. A whole flight of them. All the way to the Court of the Lions she reminded herself that the wazir couldn't possibly know she had been in the

Mirrored Room. He didn't know Suleiman wasn't a lizard anymore. Why, oh why wasn't Tahirah back?

Zoriah and Maryam stood in the courtyard looking puzzled. Layla's smile was uneasy, but she seemed calmer than Ara was feeling.

Ara walked into the lion court with Su'ah, her gaze flickering nervously about. The wazir was nowhere in sight. Maryam, dressed in a sand-colored hijab, was speaking to Zoriah. "He couldn't wait a short while? After insisting he needed to speak with my daughter and Ara, he just walked out? We dropped everything and rushed here to accommodate his wishes."

"This does seem odd," Zoriah agreed hesitantly. "He suddenly looked distracted and pale. One moment he was pacing the courtyard asking when you would arrive, a minute later he stared at the ground and abruptly rushed out."

"I've got to get back to review tonight's preparation with the servants," Maryam said, moving toward the door. "Layla, you need to finish getting ready also."

"Just a few moments, Mother. I need to speak to Ara."

"What happened?" Ara asked when the women were well out of the room.

"I'm not really sure. I got here just before he left. He was pacing, just as Zoriah said, but he stopped and seemed glued in place. Then he turned and left, completely ignoring me," Layla said with a puzzled shrug.

"Did he see something or remember he had to do something, do you think?" Ara asked, thankful she didn't have to face the evil wazir.

"He stopped when he was standing about four paces from the Lion Fountain, where the bushes are." She walked over to the spot.

"I don't see anything unusual, do you?" Ara asked.

"Not really, just dirt and pebbles and bushes," she said, looking at the ground. "Wait, what is this?" She pointed to a track

82

pushed into the soft ground. Both girls stared at a paw print, edged in red, from what looked like a very large cat.

Ara waved her hand, "This is an enclosed courtyard. Nothing gets in here. Besides, cats with paws the size of my hand don't exist. Except" —Ara turned slowly toward the stone lions, her mouth open in wonder— "for them."

Layla shuddered. "We must tell Tahirah. She'll know what it means. Maybe the lions want to help. I wanted to be brave, but I was so frightened."

"Me too," Ara agreed, thinking of her flight of butterflies. "But you looked unafraid. I think that's all we have to do."

"What, we just have to *look* brave?" Layla asked.

Ara considered. "We just have to look, well...not interested, sort of bored. The wazir doesn't know we're mixed up in this unless we tell him. Suleiman is always suspicious when I look the least bit jumpy."

Su'ah called from the arched doorway, "Ara and Layla! The People of the Book are coming up the road right now. You both need to bathe and dress. Ara, you know you have to help with translating for the women. Come, hurry along!"

"Yes, Su'ah," they replied.

Chapter 18

The evening started well enough. The wazir was busy with the sultan's work and did not seek out the two daughters of the harem.

Five of the strangers' women and three of their children had joined them for the evening meal. One lad, a bit younger than Ara with round cheeks, ginger curls and a surly expression, sat arguing with his mother. The two younger boys, dressed in velvet and silk, had the most amazing golden hair that curled at their shoulders. Ara kept stealing looks at their hair, unable to believe it was real, until Zoriah quietly pinched her and whispered, "Stop staring."

Ara looked carefully elsewhere, glad for the reminder. Layla leaned toward her, whispering, "a horizontal symmetry." And there it was, low to the ground near the floor, a flower pattern that almost crawled across the wall. Ara hugged her cousin and whispered back, "We'll find the broken one soon. We have to."

Ara's father had introduced the foreign women to his wives and female relatives and offered Ara as interpreter to them before he left to join the men. They had strange names that were hard to keep straight—Lady Anna, Lady Theresa, Lady Catalina, Sister Mary and Sister Helena. The first three were married to lords who were discussing the trade treaty with the sultan. The other two, wearing hijabs similar to Islamic women, said—or Ara thought they said—they were sisters married to Christ. It seemed unlikely, as he had been dead for some time. To make their point, they showed Ara gifts of jewelry from Him. Rosaries, they said, adorning their necks. The necklaces were made of rose petals rolled into tight balls and strung like beads. Tahirah wore a necklace that looked similar, a *tasbih*, she called it. The Sisters seemed to take great pleasure in theirs as they touched them often during dinner.

The meal was served in the Mirador de Lindaraja, a rectangular room off the Hall of the Two Sisters. It was an elegant room with low, arched windows that looked out over the countryside. Above was a stained glass ceiling that seemed to twinkle as the light penetrated it.

There was some difficulty for the Christian women as they attempted to sit down to eat. Their garments, Lady Anna explained, as she tugged impatiently at her clothes, were unsuited to sitting on the floor. After some contortions and rearranging of cushions, everyone was seated and the meal was brought in.

Course after course arrived: figs and olives to start with, then doves in pomegranate sauce, chicken with salted lemons, goat roasted with spices, eggplant sautéed and dotted with sesame seeds, fava beans with olive oil drizzled on top, carrots cooked with mint and cinnamon, and roasted almonds.

The ewers of water were the cause of some confusion as one of the women poured herself what she thought was watered wine. Ara hastily translated for Zoriah that the water was to wash their hands.

Although the guests seemed initially hesitant about some of the dishes, the banquet was going well. They admired the decorated ceramic plates on which food was served. Sister Mary explained, delicately touching the plates, that normally they used wooden trenchers and that the beauty of these surpassed any she had seen. Ara promptly passed the compliment to Zoriah, who smiled with pleasure.

Rabab was delighted with the gift of a cage full of brightly colored birds—parakeets, they were called. Lady Anna leaned over, pointing to one of the birds. It could talk, she said, but not understand. The Arab women, in return, gifted the Christians with a beautiful metal box inlaid with gold and silver designs and two large ceramic serving bowls with an opaque white glaze decorated in green and blue designs.

The ginger-haired boy, who had been complaining steadily to his mother, spit out a piece of food. Ara quickly glanced away.

All eyes drifted over to him, and all became aware that he ate with his left hand. Maryam's eyes widened; Zoriah, after a double take, looked determinedly at her plate. Ara looked anywhere but at him. Three or four servants stopped in their tracks but caught themselves after a sharp glance from Zoriah. Layla wrinkled her nose and carefully studied her food. As the smallest child knew, the left hand was for cleaning bodily functions, never for eating. Ara thanked Allah she wasn't sharing her plate with him.

Rabab was filling her plate with an eggplant dish until she too noticed the child scooping up food with his left hand. Her mouth flew open and she blurted, "That's disgusting." The foreign woman seated next to Ara smiled uncertainly and asked, "What did she say?"

Ara struggled. "She, um, she said…"

"Ara, what did she ask you?" Zoriah interrupted.

"She wants to know what Rabab said," Ara replied with a pleading look.

"Of course," Zoriah answered, nodding and smiling pleasantly at the woman. "Tell her that Rabab had an attack of indigestion, to which she is subject." Still smiling, she turned to Rabab. "You will not make another outburst."

Ara dutifully repeated Zoriah's words to Lady Anna, who smiled back but seemed unconvinced.

"What was just said?" she wanted to know.

"She was expressing concern for Rabab's health," Ara said with a straight face. Translating was more complex than she had imagined.

"Would you repeat their names for me once more?"

"The one who just spoke is Zoriah. She is Father's head wife. Next to her is Maryam, Layla's mother and my aunt. Rabab is, um, the one with digestion problems. She is my mother's mother's sister. I think you would say great aunt. Layla, my cousin and best friend, is sitting next to me, and my name is Ara."

"Thank you," Lady Anna said. "You're a very sweet child."

The ginger-haired boy raised his voice, making it hard to ignore him. "Mama, I can't eat this. I want beef, not food for dogs." He pushed his legs out to the side. "Why must we sit on the floor? I bet Father and the other men are not eating on the floor like paupers."

"Enrique, try not to fuss, dear. I know this isn't how we normally eat, but try to be pleasant. Your father has his reasons. This fall he'll make you a page. Then you'll be with the men," his mother replied, patting him on the cheek. Lady Anna, sitting next to Ara, sat rigid and turned slightly pink.

"Ara," Zoriah asked. "Is there a problem?"

Lady Anna spoke, "Ara, what did she ask?"

"She wants to know what's wrong," Ara answered uncomfortably.

"Tell her the child has a stomach ache from traveling," Lady Anna said, looking directly into her eyes.

"The boy is in poor health and misses his father," Ara translated.

"Can we get anything for him? Mint tea or a purgative?" Zoriah asked suspiciously.

Ara translated again.

"No. Thank her for her concern," Lady Anna responded before muttering under her breath. "He and I are going to have a talk. We'll be right back." She turned to Lady Theresa as she wrestled the boy out of the hall. "I'll not have your child behave this badly when we're on a delicate mission. Either you control your son or I will." As she left, her voice carried, "Enrique, mind

87

your manners right now or your father will be told of your dreadful behavior."

"What is going on?" Zoriah said, looking from one to the other.

"She asked him if he wants mint tea. He thought a walk might help," Ara ad-libbed.

Zoriah, Maryam and Rabab looked skeptically at Ara.

With Lady Anna and the ginger-haired boy's hasty departure, conversation lagged. Neither group seemed to know what to say to the other—an uncomfortable silence filled the room. The other two younger boys dutifully cleaned their plates with nary a peep. Some minutes later, a grim-faced Lady Anna reappeared with the sullen boy.

She shot him a warning glance as he jerked his arm away and sat beside his mother.

"The child feels better?" Zoriah questioned delicately.

Ara translated.

"Oh, yes, his stomach is much better, thank you," Lady Anna replied, her smile slightly forced.

Servants cleared the banquet foods, and others appeared with mint tea and dessert. Zoriah motioned Layla and Ara over.

"This would be a good time for entertainment. Ara, get your lute, please, and Layla will dance."

Ara explained to their guests that Layla would entertain them with a traditional dance, and sat down to tune her lute.

The women arranged themselves in a semicircle along the sides of the room. The boys clustered together and whispered among themselves.

Once Layla was ready, Ara started playing the music of her people. In her mind's eye, she was carried to wild windblown lands that stretched forever toward a night sky that capped them like an upside-down bowl. Stars sparkled like diamonds thrown by fistfuls up into the sky. Dark blue mountains loomed in the distance. A herd of camels huddled together against the cold of the dark desert evening. She heard a camel call that dissolved into the ginger haired boy's snort.

He pointed at Layla and snorted again with laughter. She looked up to see if any adults noticed. Didn't look like it. Zoriah and Maryam were smiling at Layla as she danced. Rabab's eyes were closed and her mouth gaped slightly. Asleep again. Lady Anna was smiling and gently tapping her knee in time to the music. Christ's wives and other ladies were watching with polite but uncomfortable expressions on their faces. Ara ducked her head and continued playing, fiercely concentrating on her music.

She heard the boy's snort once again and almost lost a beat. He whispered loudly to the golden-haired boys, "Look at the way she wiggles."

Ara gritted her teeth and kept playing, her grip on the lute neck tightened as thoughts of throttling one ginger-haired infidel consumed her. Father would be at war, the Alhambra would be lost—all because she attacked a pudgy boy. Allah would understand.

In her fury, Ara missed the white-robed figure who stood quietly observing at the entryway.

She snuck an angry look at the boy and was startled to see he had a slingshot pulled taut and pointed at Layla. She dropped her lute and shouted, "No." Too late, she knew. The slingshot snapped and ricocheted back. The boy was hit smack in his mouth. He screamed; several adults leaped to his aid. Lady Anna walked over with a grim look and picked up the broken slingshot, displaying it to the mother trying to calm her howling boy. The other Christians were distressed and then angry as they deciphered the situation. One of Christ's wives started fingering the beads in her rosary.

Maryam stood protectively by her daughter. Zoriah seemed unsure quite how to react. Rabab was now awake and confused. And Allah's blessing upon them, Tahirah stood in the doorway, calmly surveying the scene.

Lady Anna spoke first, trembling in rage. "The boy will be punished, I assure you."

Tahirah glanced thoughtfully at the boy's bloodied nose and lip, before saying in her perfect Castilian Spanish, "I believe Justice has already been provided."

Chapter 19

Later that evening, Layla and Ara met Tahirah walking through the torch-lit halls; their long shadows moved with them across the walls.

"We're so glad you are back," Layla stated, her face still a bit pale.

"Where were you?" Ara asked at the same time.

Tahirah reached out and took their hands in hers. "It has been quite the experience for all of us." She gave their hands a squeeze before releasing them. "I dreaded leaving you two, but I received an urgent message from an old friend, a woman from Lindejarras in the mountains. I left immediately, taking only my guards and two of my most trusted women." Ara leaned forward. "When I arrived, she spoke of a plot to overthrow the Alhambra."

Both girls gasped.

"My friend's brother travels in a caravan across Andalusia. She told me that two months ago, three knights from Seville joined their caravan. Late that night, he heard them arguing. They were disagreeing about a Muslim wazir in the service of the Castilian king. This wazir was supposed to have magic, they said, that could strip the palace of its defenses so that the Alhambra would drop into their hands like a ripe fig.

"Two of these men didn't trust the wazir or his magic, and wanted to take the matters into their own hands, but the other man persuaded them to let the 'Moor undo the Alhambra magic,' then kill him. My friend's brother wanted to warn the sultan, but he was afraid."

"Why would the wazir do this?" Layla asked.

"According to the knights, the wazir has been promised the Alhambra for his own if Granada falls to the Infidels."

"I don't understand, how could the Alhambra be made defenseless? We have guards and soldiers," Ara persisted.

Tahirah reached out to stroke Ara's hair. She spoke gently. "The Alhambra is protected by people, it is true, but you know that the secret of its strength is in the magic built into its walls by the original Moors and Saracens. They placed the magic in the artwork, the symmetry on the walls themselves, and that protects the palace from invaders. With the magic intact, these fortress walls cannot be breached, the gates are impenetrable, and the towers themselves will resonate like thunder. Lightning bolts would shoot any hostile army that dared to trespass."

"That's what Father was talking about," Ara said, placing a hand on the walls as if she could hold it together by herself. "He said that the Alhambra protects its own."

Tahirah looked solemn. "If all the symmetries broke, the magic would be undone, and the Alhambra would be like any other palace. No number of warriors and guards could defend it from superior forces.

"The symmetries hold, in spite of the fault line of evil spreading throughout the walls and weakening its magic. But if we are unsuccessful, the damage will continue and eventually the fortress will fall."

"And the lions—what do they do?" Ara asked. "You said that they are magic."

"The lions were set into place by three very powerful mathemagicians hundreds of years ago. Each lion was named for a quality that would protect the Alhambra. Their anger would be terrible and inescapable for any who endangers the Red Palace. Their continued silence concerns me, and I must assume the worst. The wazir has placed a spell on them. When you broke that first binding on Suleiman, some of the evil was dispelled."

Ara's eyes widened with urgency. "Tahirah, we saw a lion's footprint on the ground this morning."

"The wazir saw it too." Layla interrupted, her words tumbling over one another in her hurry to get them out. "He was going to ask us about Suleiman, but he left in a rush when he saw the lion's print."

Tahirah weighed this information before speaking. "The wazir must be very frightened. His control of the lions has slipped, and his magic is unraveling." She frowned and pressed her fingers to her mouth. "We must be cautious. He must not guess you two are responsible for his magic weakening."

She resumed walking. "If we only had some written proof, we could go to your father. As it is, it would be my word against his, and this is a very serious accusation. Islamic law requires the voice of two women for every man." Her voice cracked. "I would not accuse the wazir of treason with no more than hearsay."

She remained quiet for some moments, then said, "As I watched the moon change each night, I thought of you two. This morning it was just past a quarter full. What have you accomplished while I was gone?"

The girls looked at each other, then at their hands. Ara whispered, "We have yet to find a broken horizontal symmetry, and we must by tomorrow." She sent an anxious glance toward Layla.

Tahirah nodded and was silent. She closed her eyes and for a few minutes she seemed to be meditating.

Her eyes snapped open and she said, "Tomorrow is a busy day. You are translating for the visitors, are you not?"

Both girls nodded yes.

"Then I bid you goodnight. But remember, fear is not our friend, and we will not feed him. This evening I need to spend in solitude and prayer, but perhaps I can help before I go. As I entered the Alhambra tonight, I saw the wazir alone in a room off the Gilded Court. Did you check near there?"

"We'll go now," Ara said, pulling Layla along with her. "Quickly, before bedtime."

"Good night, daughters of my heart," Tahirah called quietly after them.

They ran through the palace, stopping only to nod politely to others of the harem as they passed. Guards stood at various corners, untouched by the apparent enthusiasms of the youngsters. Children had been running through the halls of the Alhambra long before these two were born.

As they were about to round the last corner, Ara pointed to a row of tiles surrounding the doorway. "I think...No, there's a piece that changes the symmetry, an extra shape in the top half that is not in the bottom, not a symmetry, but not broken. Oh, bother," she muttered under her breath, glancing around at other tiles. She had to find the symmetry. What would happen to her father and all her family and friends if she did not? The sound of strange male voices raised in anger came from around the corner. The girls looked at each other in surprise. Who could be in the Gilded Court at this hour of the night?

"What do you mean the palace is healing itself?" a voice barked. "You told me it was all under control. Can't do your simple math magics?" The speaker laughed at his own joke.

"Keep your voice down," the wazir said jumpily. "Do you want everyone to hear? The sultan is already suspicious. He questions me closely about my relations with you of Castile.

"The symmetries are healing, and the lions are casting off the sleep spell I placed on them. Someone is working against me. That eunuch, Suleiman, I'm sure. Somehow, even in his reptilian form, he's doing mathemagics."

More laughter. "A lizard doing math," the voice sneered. "What's he doing, trigonometry?"

Ara could hear the intake of the wazir's breath.

The man continued, seemingly unaware of the wazir's anger. "What about that woman, the Sufi?"

The wazir laughed and whispered in his harsh voice, "A woman, an old woman. Sufis spend their lives thinking great thoughts. Tahirah's weak. She wouldn't even *notice* the changes, much less be able to fix them. It must be the eunuch. He was sniffing around my magic. I should have killed him."

94

"We're not interested in your bizarre excuses," the other man went on. "If we don't see progress, and soon, you may not be as valuable to the King of Castile as you think."

"Keep your voice down, I tell you," the wazir repeated. "You want the whole palace up in arms? I said I would hand you the key to the Alhambra, and I shall. Look here, see the pattern? Watch as I break it."

Ara and Layla held tightly to each other. Ara felt a gut-wrenching pull as the wazir's magic tugged at the Alhambra.

"See, another symmetry broken. My magic doesn't fail me. You infidels are so easily discouraged. I grow stronger and persevere. Don't underestimate me, knight," the wazir said, gathering back his confidence.

"Islamic boor. I should kill you now and be done with it," the Christian growled.

"Fool, I have more power in my little finger than you and that Spanish stick you call a sword can muster." A pop sounded and smoke drifted around the corner. "Take this to your lord as a reminder: never threaten a mathemagician."

"My feet!" The words were a wail. "*Ay Dios mio!* I have hooves like a donkey," the knight shrieked. "What evil have you done? I'll kill you for this." Ara heard a clip clopping that echoed in the room.

"Not if you ever wish to be whole again." The wazir laughed. "Return to your people. Let them know who is powerful here."

Ara reached trembling fingers to Layla and yanked, motioning her to retreat back down the hallway. Silently, they crept, holding their breath, afraid that at any moment the wazir would come striding down the hall. When they were far enough away, they bolted for their room.

Chapter 20

The next morning, Ara woke with a start. She had slept uneasily, dreaming of being chased by a Christian-garbed donkey with an evil grin upon his face.

Layla still slept; a wary look flittered across her face. As usual, Su'ah was awake and puttering about, building up the fire and laying out their clothes. Ara rolled out of bed.

"Up early, are you?" Su'ah asked. "You must have had quite the fright. I heard about that horrible boy. Why would anyone want to hurt Layla? The servants overheard the commotion in the guest quarters last night. His father was most displeased. That child won't be sitting down for some time." She leaned out of the window to shake dust from a carpet. In the distance, a rooster crowed.

"Su'ah, would you mind walking with me this morning? I need to go down to the Gilded Hall, and I don't wish to go alone," Ara asked, nervous of a chance confrontation with the wazir.

"Now?"

"I need to find something. It won't take long. It's important, and I really am a bit afraid to go alone," she insisted.

Su'ah sighed and looked around at all the work still to be done. With a small shake of her head, she conceded, "Of course, child. I understand. If my aged company would give you comfort, I would be pleased to go. There are too many strangers wandering these halls. And that undisciplined boy. He wouldn't have behaved like that had he been in my charge," she continued with an emphatic nod of her head. "I know how to raise a well-mannered child."

Together, they walked down the stairs and through the Court of the Myrtles before heading into the Gilded Court.

"My, my, someone brought an animal in here." Su'ah frowned at the hoof prints. "Look at that floor. Hoof prints all

96

over. Zoriah won't be pleased that livestock was brought into the hall. I had better call a servant to mop this up."

She stopped a passing slave-girl and spoke to her, pointing at the offending scuffmarks. Ara took the opportunity to scoot past a large urn and into a small alcove.

"Ara, where are you?"

"Over here," she called out as she peered through an arched doorway. She searched the walls from top to bottom. Only a single sad twisted tile remained from the wazir's magic, but not a horizontal symmetry.

"Soon all will be well," she whispered, touching it gently. She turned toward Su'ah. "I'm ready to go."

"What were you looking for? Did you tell me before? My mind isn't as sharp as it once was," Su'ah lamented, shaking her head.

"I thought I left a lute string in here last week, but I don't see it," Ara said, uncomfortable at deceiving her, but she knew how Su'ah liked to talk. If word got back to the wazir that she searched for symmetries, broken symmetries...she cringed at the thought.

"Child, you'd lose your hand if it weren't attached. Let's go back, I'm sure we can find another lute string. I have to get you and Layla off to the baths, dressed and ready for the day's meeting with those foreigners."

Su'ah frowned. "Now, you remember, if that boy even looks at you oddly, you come tell your old Su'ah and I'll deal with him myself." She puffed herself up like a hen preparing to defend her chicks.

Ara smiled, thinking about Su'ah and the ginger-haired boy. She would bet on Su'ah every time. She slowed her pace to match hers as they walked back up to their sleeping quarters. "Must we join them this morning?" she asked. "Even after what happened with Layla?"

"I wasn't told either way, but you must be ready and willing if your father deems it so," Su'ah reproved. "He is the sultan. His word is law."

Layla was awake and up by the time they returned, curious where they had gone so early in the morning. Her eyes widened at Ara when Su'ah told her where they had been.

"Did you find what you were looking for?" she asked.

Ara shook her head, reminding Layla to keep silent. "I didn't see the lute string."

Su'ah began grumbling again. "Hoof prints in the courtyard! Some hooligan brought a horse or donkey into the Gilded Court. I hope no one saw this and thinks we live like that. Maybe the Infidels let livestock into their homes, but not in this palace!" She hesitated at the door. "You girls head off to the baths, and don't dawdle now."

Layla finished putting on her sandals before addressing her cousin. "Ara, today's our last day to find the horizontal symmetry, right?"

"Yes, but we'll find it," Ara said, thinking to reassure her.

"That's not what I was thinking about." She paused. "What will Suleiman change into the next time?"

Confused at her cousin's line of thought, Ara shrugged. "I don't know, another animal of some sort."

"Yes, but we have him in my embroidery basket. What if he turns into an elephant and runs trumpeting through the palace. Or a bee and wanders off into the gardens or worse, a fish?" "There are many things he could turn into and disappear or die. We might never find him."

Ara looked at Layla in dawning horror. Why hadn't she thought of that before? Both girls sat on the floor and frowned.

"Well, we'd better keep the basket close to us and try *not* to find this broken symmetry when other people are around, just in case," Ara agreed, trying to think where she could hide an elephant.

"Let's go bathe and get dressed. Maybe we'll be lucky and he will be something small, cute and cuddly this time," Layla said hopefully. She checked on the still-sleeping Suleiman before taking up his basket. They gathered the rest of their things and walked down to the baths.

"At least the People of the Book leave today," Ara said to lift their mood. "I'll be happy to see that ginger-haired boy go. I do like Lady Anna though; she is nice and smells of lavender."

"Me too. Have you heard how the talks are going? Mother says a treaty could help keep the peace between us and the Christians."

"Father is still angry with me. I haven't seen him at all." Ara bit her cheek. She missed the comfort of her father's smile. "In any case, we need to prevent the wazir from undoing the Alhambra's magic. Treaty or no treaty, the Castile King might decide to claim Granada."

"Couldn't Tahirah do some magic to stop him? Turn him into a toad or something?"

"A Sufi's magic is in learning and knowledge. Because she is a Sufi, she can do good, but she can't harm others. That would be evil in the eyes of Allah," Ara said, remembering a discussion from her teachers. "Though I wondered about that slingshot breaking just as she came into the room, didn't you?"

Chapter 21

Maryam hurried toward them as the cousins headed back up the stairs. They had bathed and dressed and felt ready to face the world once again.

"I've been looking for you two. The sultan needs you to join us for breakfast. The Christians are leaving this morning. Not soon enough for me, "" she added, recalling last night's upset. "But soon. Lady Anna asked your father if you would translate for her again." A small smile escaped Maryam's hold on her expression. "I have been told that Lady Theresa's son will not be dining with us today. He has been afflicted with some slight ailment, one that makes it difficult for him to sit. Nothing catching, I understand." She winked.

Ara groaned; she had hoped to avoid their guests. Layla gave her mother a crooked smile. "I'm to go also?"

"Yes, the foreign women were embarrassed by yesterday's incident, and they wish to make amends. It would be a courtesy if you allowed them that opportunity," Maryam said. "I was pleased with the way both of you handled yourselves last night. You two helped prevent a dispute between us and the foreigners."

She grabbed her hijab and slid it over her head. "Come, we must go over to the Kings' Hall and join our company."

At the look from the girls, she explained, "Many men will be attending, and I don't want to feel naked before them. Soon you also will wear a hijab, but that time is not yet."

Maryam's eyes developed an impish twinkle. "I hesitate to mention this, but recently that embroidery basket is always with you. I never see the two of you without it. Ara, don't tell me you've suddenly become fascinated with embroidery?"

Both girls looked at one another and then the basket. Ara was the first to recover. "Zoriah is concerned with my skill at sewing. Layla's been helping me to work on my stitches. Her basket has more room in it to carry things."

Maryam looked at the two girls and raised one eyebrow.

Ara thought the basket on her arm must shine like a beacon, drawing unwanted attention as they walked along. She and Layla tried to act casually, pointedly not looking at the basket. Instead, she forced herself to stare at the arched doorway coming up. A broken horizontal symmetry leapt out at her, and it writhed before her eyes, healing. A chorus of roars reverberated through the Alhambra. Ara stopped to listen, but before she could identify where the noise came from, the basket jerked. A rousing thump and a squeak came from inside it. Maryam looked at the basket and then at the girls.

"I...I have to go outside," Ara stammered.

Layla edged toward the gardens. "I'll go with her. We'll be right back."

"I think that might be best," Maryam agreed with an amused smile. "And before you return, make sure any animals that might be in the basket are released outside."

The girls turned and ran.

"What happened?" Layla asked. "I thought we were trying not to find the broken symmetry until we were alone."

"I didn't mean to," Ara explained, hurrying out the door. "It was just there! Now what are we going to do? Your mother knows we have something in the basket. She thinks we're going to let it go, and we can't."

"We'll have to carry him without the basket," Layla said. She raised her eyes toward Allah. "Please, let him be cute and cuddly this time."

They carefully lifted the lid of the basket and peered inside. Layla jumped and then wrinkled her nose as she always did when displeased.

"Oh, no." Ara sighed. "Well, at least he's small."

A plain brown, rather chubby mouse stared up at them. "I'm hungry," he squeaked plaintively.

"Not now, Suleiman," Ara said. "We have to go to the Kings' Hall. We'll feed you later. Here, climb onto my hand and you can hide in my sleeve. We can't hide you in my basket anymore—Layla's mother is suspicious. Just don't move around. I'm ticklish."

"Rice," Suleiman squeaked as he scrabbled onto Ara's outstretched palm.

"What?" the girls said together.

"That's what I eat," he announced, sitting straight up and staring determinedly at Ara. "You didn't feed me the whole time I was a snake," he added in an aggrieved tone of voice.

Ara brought her hand up to eye level and carefully stroked the mouse across the head with the tip of her finger. "Suleiman, you've got to be patient. We must go back to my aunt now. She's waiting for us. Food has to wait."

"But I hunger," his slightly muffled squeak insisted again as Ara pushed him up her sleeve until he was hidden in the folds of her caftan.

He disappeared without further protest, and Layla sighed in relief. "We can figure out where to keep him as soon as the Northerners leave. I sure hope it's soon."

Ara turned in a small circle. "Did you hear that sound before? I thought I heard lions roaring."

"No, nothing. Could it have been voices echoing from outside?"

"Perhaps."

They hurried back inside, where Layla's mother waited with growing impatience. "I assume you girls have resolved the basket problem."

"Yes, Mother. I don't think it will be a problem again," Layla said, blushing slightly at her mother's disapproving voice.

Ara said nothing, very conscious of the tickling whiskers at her elbow.

"Then let us go." Maryam urged the girls ahead with her hands as she walked. "We are running late."

The murals adorning the ceiling of the Hall of the Kings always fascinated Ara. No geometric shapes above them. She wondered who had painted these pictures so unlike the art in the rest of the palace. Pictures of kings and their court looked down from above them. Knights and damsels moved above in lifelike splendor. A wild-eyed man, clearly crazy, decorated one panel. He stood frozen, forever holding a bloodied sword. Ara deliberated on that picture, trembling at how much he reminded her of the wazir. The room was crowded: women in tightly fitted, low cut dresses and funny pointed hats; women unseen inside their hijabs with dark eyes shining out. Men wearing turbans and long beards, and men bareheaded with tightly trimmed beards. Seeing living people of both cultures mixed together shook her for a minute, a replica of the ceiling. She blinked her eyes and refocused.

Breakfast was being cleared from the long low table. The wazir was standing behind her father, a vexed look upon his face. Her father sat surrounded by his advisors and two of the Christian ambassadors. Papers for the trade agreement were laid out before them; a discussion seemed to be going on. Her father glanced up at her from his chair as she walked in. At a flick of his fingers, a servant rushed to her side. "His Eminence, may Allah protect him, has requested that you sit by the Lady Anna."

"Tell my father that I am honored. *Alhamdulillah*," Ara replied formally as she joined the others at the table. Layla and her mother sat next to Zoriah, farther down.

"Ara." Lady Anna smiled up at her. "I was hoping you would join us this morning. Would you care for something before all the food is removed, or have you already eaten?"

"I'm not very hungry." A nip on her elbow startled her. "Oh, wait, maybe a little food would be nice."

Ara tucked her feet under her as she sat next to Lady Anna. Tahirah, dressed in her white woolen cloak, was caught up in an animated discussion with the sisters who were Christ's wives. She glanced at Ara for a split second before refocusing on her conversation.

Lady Anna fidgeted uneasily before speaking. "I wanted to thank you for your kindnesses last night and assure you that Enrique has been firmly reprimanded. I was much relieved that your lovely cousin was not harmed. Enrique was showing off for the other boys, and it got a little out of control."

"It was my honor and privilege," Ara replied, embarrassed at how eagerly she had wished for them to leave. Another sharp nip reminded her of her hidden companion. A tray of pilaf sat an arm's length away. She scooped some onto a plate and ate unhurriedly, "accidentally" dropping a few grains of rice into her lap. Her left arm rested unseen beneath the table. Suleiman began inching his way out of her sleeve, trying to reach a grain of rice just beyond his grasp.

The sultan stood, and all attention turned to him. "This has been a great moment in history. Our cultures have come together to establish mutually beneficial trade agreements and resolve crucial boundary issues. We have worked to dismiss age-old conflicts and start anew. As an outcome of this meeting, Christians and Muslims and Jews shall continue to live in peace and prosperity, *inshallah*."

The Aragon ambassador stood. Before speaking, he bowed politely to the sultan and thanked him for his hospitality, expressing his desire for peace and prosperity. Several other Northern dignitaries came forward and bowed, trotting out their own speeches. But Ara watched others. Not everyone was pleased. The wazir and the Castilian liaison huddled together, words whispered between them.

Finally, the meeting was over. The Northerners bowed once again before turning to leave. The wazir hurried to the sultan's side, attaching himself like a blood-sucking leech. Ara dug her fingernails into her hands with worry. He was up to something. Something with the Castilians.

Zoriah tapped her shoulder, and Ara jumped. She rapidly translated, summarizing the speeches for the women.

Finally, it was over. Lady Anna thanked Ara, holding her hand tightly before she stood and signaled her companions that it was time to depart.

Ara, after furtively pushing Suleiman back inside her sleeve, rose to her feet. A small squeak of dismay came from her sleeve.

Lady Anna looked at Ara in surprise. "Did you say something?"

"No, just a burp of pleasure," Ara said, blushing furiously as she walked with their guests. Servants and slaves of both Christians and Muslims gathered, helping to move luggage and boxes onto the waiting carts.

Ara watched them depart, waving to the Lady Anna as she disappeared through the Gate of Justice. The sultan retired to his private rooms to review the outcome of the two-day meeting. The wazir remained outside.

The women of the harem celebrated with an ululating call, and Layla danced around in glee that the meeting had gone well and was over. Suleiman hung on for dear life in Ara's sleeve. She moved to the window, watching the wazir and wondering what he was plotting.

As they left the Hall, Tahirah walked alongside Zoriah, "Now that I have returned, I would like to continue the girls' lessons. I hope that they are available later this day."

Zoriah raised her eyebrows in surprise. "You just returned. Surely you are exhausted from your journey. The children can wait; your well-being is more important." As an afterthought, she added, "Are the girls badgering you? I know they missed you, but I don't want them imposing on your kind nature."

Tahirah laughed. "No, not at all. I agreed to see to their lessons, and then I set them adrift. I enjoy these two. Their company has been Allah's gift to me."

"What are you teaching them?" Zoriah asked after a short pause in the conversation.

"We are exploring mathematics and science. With students as bright and attentive as Ara and Layla, education almost plots its own course."

"Interesting," Zoriah said with a perplexed look in her eyes. "You're certainly welcome to start the girls' lessons any time you wish. The sultan is pleased that they are getting so remarkable an instructor. I'll tell Su'ah to send them to your rooms, but let me know if you change your mind and want some peace and quiet."

Tahirah smiled quietly. "I believe the girls and I will do quite well together, *inshallah*."

Chapter 22

"Where is Suleiman?" Layla worriedly asked as Ara struggled to remove her caftan.

"He's in here somewhere. He moved up my sleeve and won't stay still." Angrily, Ara reached behind her head. "I'm going to grab him by his tail and..." A loud, prolonged squeak came from behind her.

"You're squooshing me," the mouse shrieked, wriggling deeper in her hair. Layla gently tried to remove the mouse from the tangle.

"Stop being a baby," Ara yelled back, flapping her hands at the back of her head. "You should have stayed where I put you— ouch, that hurt!"

"Ara, be still," Layla said as she disentangled the upset mouse from the equally upset girl. "He keeps wiggling and you keep wiggling. Stop it. You're both making it worse." Ara held her hands determinedly at her side while Layla worked.

"There!" Layla triumphantly cupped the offended looking mouse in her hand. "He's free."

"Girls, what's all that racket?" Su'ah called as she shambled into the room. Her eyes widened in disbelief. "Ara, what did you do to your hair? I had it so neatly braided. I don't understand how you get messy so quickly." She went over to the girls, hairbrush in hand. "It looks like a rat's nest. What have you done this time?" Evaluating the devastation, she added, "Even for you, this is remarkable."

Layla and Ara looked at one another guiltily. Layla placed the palmed mouse in her sleeve and, smiling sheepishly, began, "We were in a hurry and Ara, um, Ara—" she began.

"I thought I felt a bee in my hair," Ara finished.

"You were in a hurry, and you felt a bee in your hair," Su'ah repeated, slowly looking from girl to girl. There was silence while she mulled over their story, a frown on her face while she tugged the brush through Ara's long black hair with well-practiced strokes, patiently stopping to unsnarl each knot. "Well, I suppose that's as believable as many of your stories," she concluded. "Tahirah wants you in her rooms. You'd better get a move on. Her servants are waiting outside for you."

"Allah be praised," Ara muttered and started to pull away, but Su'ah pulled back.

"Not this moment," she amended. "Let me finish braiding your hair. At least you'll start out tidy. Bees, hmm." She yanked Ara's braid a bit harder than seemed necessary.

As soon as Su'ah was satisfied that Ara was presentable once again, the girls rushed out of the room. Tahirah's servants were hard put to keep up with them in their eagerness to tell her of Suleiman's latest transformation.

"We only have five and one quarter days from when he changed into a mouse," whispered Layla. "I wonder what the next pattern of symmetry we have to find is?"

Tahirah was crouched, working with something on the floor when they entered. A servant followed behind them bringing in steaming lemon tea. "Thank you," Tahirah said to the woman, who bowed respectfully upon leaving.

"We have much work to do," Tahirah said over her shoulder to the girls, "and little time. I felt a healing in the fabric of the Alhambra this morning. You must have found horizontal symmetry, the broken one."

Ara nodded and came closer, saying excitedly, "Look, Suleiman's changed into a mouse." Layla carefully set the rodent on Tahirah's shoulder.

The mathemagician tensed and slowly turned her head to stare as the mouse busily cleaned his whiskers and smoothed down his fur. "I am grateful the spell is unraveling," she said slowly, "but there are other animals I would have been more pleased to see." There was a long pause before Tahirah finished flatly, "Mice bring back very bad memories for me."

"But, I thought you weren't afraid of anything," Layla burst out, shocked, and quickly cupped the mouse into her hand.

"Everyone is afraid of something. Some more than others," Tahirah said slowly, still watching the mouse. "Most of my family died from the Black Death. The plague came and whole villages died." Her eyes had a faraway look. "It isn't a pleasant death. Some said it was Allah's will, but I knew it was not. Allah is only joy and beauty. There was neither joy nor beauty in this.

"I was very young, a year or so younger than the two of you, and just learning the power of mathemagics. The plague passed me by, but I was unable to save my family.

"Thousands of people died that year. No one was safe, from the lowest of the low to sultans in their walled palaces. All died. And always, the rats and mice were there, hundreds and thousands of them, crawling over everything. They died too. Everything died." She shuddered and took a breath.

The girls stood transfixed, unsure how to react, while Tahirah continued to wrestle with her memories.

Suleiman looked up from polishing his whiskers. "What?" he asked. His sharp black eyes alighted on the tray of flat bread, fruit and olives. "Is that bread? I'm very hungry."

Tahirah rubbed her hand across her forehead and slowly the expression on her face changed. "Suleiman, I say to you what I say to others, 'whithersoever ye turn, there is the Face of God.' Once again, Allah shows me the folly of my ways. I accept and learn. Food you may have and the support of my hand and heart, may I ever be Allah's vessel, *inshallah*."

Ara leapt in. "He's really little, and he won't hurt anyone. I'm sorry about your family, truly I am, Tahirah."

"Child, that was ages ago. I thought I had put it far behind me. This has reminded me that goodness comes in all shapes, not just the ones I like." She took one last calming breath. "Time for us to continue. Suleiman, please sup. You must be hungry. Then you and I will teach the next symmetry pattern," she added firmly, pulling herself together.

The mouse leapt off Layla's arm and scampered over to the bread. Tahirah and the girls sat down to their tea. The girls sipped from their cups, quieter than usual, afraid to disturb their friend and teacher. Suleiman, after muttering a polite *bismillah*, ate some bread, then exclaimed in delight upon finding a ripe fig. He devoured a large mouse-mouthful.

"Tea is calming, is it not?" Tahirah said, smiling at the girls. "I believe it is time, perhaps even past time, for our next lesson. Suleiman, I hope you are now full and ready."

The mouse looked up, cheeks stuffed with food. After some internal debate, he finally mumbled, "Uff courshh," and swallowing, joined the group.

Tahirah pointed behind her to a stack of ceramic tiles on the floor. "I searched out some tiles for our lesson. This will make it easier to explain and not use expensive paper. As you remember, your last symmetry was a horizontal reflection. And the one before that was a vertical reflection." She paused. Suleiman had scurried over to the tiles and was running around each one. "I instructed you to find the horizontal symmetry, making absolutely sure that it did not also have a vertical symmetry."

"Yes, we were very careful about that. You said it was important," Ara recalled. Layla nodded.

"This third symmetry has *both* a vertical and a horizontal reflection. Both symmetries exist in one design. That's why it was important not to find a vertical symmetry with the horizontal one last time. Let us put together some of the tiles to make this pattern."

Suleiman, who had been carefully examining the tiles,

placed a paw on some. "Here, this is the first example I showed you, a triangle," he squeaked. "Take these four tiles and make a design that has both vertical and horizontal reflections."

Ara and Layla sat down near the tiles. This didn't look too hard. Layla reached to pick up a tile and then looked at Ara, who nodded encouragement.

Layla left the first tile alone and slid the second directly below it and turned it until the blue was on the bottom. The next two tiles she placed on the right side. One she placed white edges

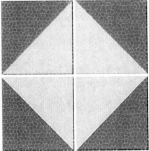

matching with the top one, and the other she slid under to match.

She looked up at Tahirah when she was finished. "Is this correct?" she sounded uncertain.

"Perfect, though there are other answers. Now explain why it is correct," Tahirah encouraged, pleased that shy Layla was attempting this problem.

The girl lay on her stomach, studying the tiles. "Well, the two on the top are the flips of each other...and the tiles below look exactly like a mirror reflection of the ones above." She hesitated then, less confident. "But mathematics isn't really this easy, is it? It's always been hard for me. Ara is the one who likes math."

Tahirah thought for a second before responding. "It can be simple. Mathematics is a human way of explaining the world. It gives us some insight into the wonders that Allah created. Part of the world is very simple, and part is more complex.

"The basics of mathematics are very easy. Complex mathematics is only the basics added together, step by step. Each step is not complex, though the whole may seem that way.

"It's as dance is for you, Layla, or playing the lute for Ara. Placing your finger on a string and plucking a note is not hard, but playing a tune takes much practice. Playing many tunes well takes again more practice. Mathematics also takes practice. You are learning to think in different ways and, as you do, it becomes easier." She smiled down at the girls. Suleiman climbed upon Layla's back to get a better view and surveyed the scene with the air of a miniature ruler.

Tahirah, though still uncomfortable with the mouse, pressed on stalwartly. "Here is a more complex example of the double reflection we are studying."

Ara touched the tile. "I've seen this. It's in the Hall of the Two Sisters. I never noticed the symmetry of it before."

"Yes, it's a copy of the one on the far left wall as you enter. It is very lovely, is it not?" Tahirah said, admiring the tile maker's work. "One more point I need to make with this symmetry is that it looks the same right-side up or upside down."

Layla screwed up her nose. Ara also looked unsure. "You mean if you turn the tile upside down, it still looks the same?" Ara said, turning the piece around. "Oh. It *is* the same. How odd."

"That's it?" Layla's smile was hesitant. "Just if it's the same when it's upside down as right side up?"

"Yes." Tahirah agreed, smiling, as she took out more tiles. "Now make this pattern into a band or row."

Ara took two more identical tiles and lined them up edge to edge with the first.

"Good. If you look you can see that the reflections in the row are a bit different from the single tile. The row has only one horizontal flip but there are multiple places within the row where there is a vertical flip. You could put a mirror between each tile and it would reflect, or you could put a mirror straight down the exact center of a tile and it would also reflect."

"Yes," Ara exclaimed, catching on. "There are many places where it could be folded in half and match exactly."

"I have said that you two almost teach yourselves, and it is very true," Tahirah said with pleasure.

They stood, grinning at the praise, and prepared to leave, Suleiman hidden again in the folds of Layla's sleeve.

Ara suddenly leaned forward and said in a near whisper. "The wazir. We heard the wazir talking. He knows his evil spells are unraveling, and he searches for Suleiman."

"We heard he still believes that Suleiman is a lizard," Layla said, "but he thinks Suleiman is somehow undoing his magic."

Tahirah frowned. "We have been fortunate, have we not? The wazir searches for the one who thwarts him in his magic. He is arrogant and blind and hasn't yet turned his eye toward the harem. I have placed spells about the palace to avert his interest from us. How long they will last, I cannot say." There was silence in the room except for Suleiman's anxious breathing. "Allah forbid that he learn of your involvement.

"Every day that he is unaware of your connection to the magic is a day we rejoice. I count each as a blessing from Allah." She bowed her head. Seconds passed while Tahirah regained her composure.

"You have less time yet again, only five and one quarter days, and much of this day has vanished with our Christian guests. But all is not lost; the People of the Book are gone, and no more beet juice must be cleaned from the lion fountain," she added with a wry smile.

Ara shook herself out of her fear. "Wait, before we leave. Can we use this same symmetry? The one from the Hall of the Two Sisters? Does it count?"

"The magic works as long as you see a broken symmetry, one that in your heart you are seeking. Be very careful whom you ask for help. A secret is no longer a secret when two people know," she warned. "This lesson is over, so off with you. Remember, courage outweighs fear." Opening the door, she waved them out of the room.

Chapter 23

The sun was low in the sky when the girls, accompanied by four guards, left Tahirah's rooms. Worried about finding the newest symmetry, they entered the Palace of the Myrtles and headed for their chambers, searching the walls as they walked.

Zoriah, surrounded by seven servants, called to them from the top of the stairs, "Are you girls done with your lesson?"

"Yes, but we have assignments to complete for it."

Zoriah turned away from them to one servant, who hovered attentively. "No, it can't be done tomorrow," she told her impatiently. "I want the rugs cleaned now. "She turned back to the girls. "And I want you to go and make sure that the Mirador de Lindaraja is completely cleaned."

"Now?" Ara questioned in surprise. "Us?"

"Yes, now and definitely you." Zoriah's voice sounded exasperated. "How do you expect to learn the running of a castle if you don't start while you're young? You can't tell servants and slaves how to do something if you haven't done it yourself. Now, go with the servants and help them get the rooms in order."

Ara and Layla looked at each other in dismay. They were tired and Suleiman still hid in Layla's sleeve. Each hour they didn't find a symmetry was an hour lost forever. The wazir knew something was wrong—what if he looked to those who were close to him? He might guess they were involved.

Ara couldn't speak.

"Of course, Zoriah," Layla finally answered.

As they left the hall, Ara muttered under her breath, annoyed at Zoriah and frightened of what could happen.

"You know she's right. We have to learn," Layla said quietly, so the accompanying servants, ahead, wouldn't hear.

"But not now," Ara snapped. "We have no time. What if we fail? Neither of us sleep at night for worrying."

"She doesn't know that, and we can't tell her," Layla said, hurt.

"But the wazir is doing something with the Castilians. I know he is."

Layla placed her hand on her cousin's shoulder. "Nothing we can do will change that. We must stick to our task, repairing the Alhambra and Suleiman with it."

Ara sighed and then shuddered as a new thought crossed her mind. "What if the wazir connects us with Suleiman's disappearance and comes looking for us?"

Ara watched as her own fear bloomed in Layla's eyes.

The girls climbed upstairs to their room, both too tired to talk. Cleaning and scrubbing, airing carpets and polishing floors had taken hours. Zoriah had checked before they had finished and suggested that the kitchen staff could use help the next day with counting a shipment of food that had just arrived. It had been a *long* evening. As they stumbled into bed, Ara fervently hoped Zoriah would find some other girls to take under her wing and train. She wasn't sure she would survive her lessons.

The next day, servants joined them directly after breaking fast, and the girls followed them to their tasks. The evening ended as the previous one, with both girls falling into bed exhausted.

Morning dawned before they felt they had even closed their eyes. The voices of the muezzins rang out the call to prayer.

"I'm sore all over," Ara protested as she slowly pushed off the bedcovers. "I thought we were done with scrubbing and polishing and cleaning when the Christians left."

"And counting jars and jars of olive oil," Layla added, recalling the previous day tallying the large shipment unloaded from the wagon.

"Break fast time!" chimed a shrill voice near Ara's ear. Suleiman clambered off her pillow and skittered over to the bed's edge. "Hurry, get up. We need to eat."

Ara eyed the mouse with sleepy annoyance. "Can't you think of anything but your stomach?"

Suleiman turned and drew his portly mouse-self up to his full height. "Of course, there are many things of equal importance as one's health. One is treating your elders properly. You are a girl and I..."

"Are a mouse."

Layla, ever the peacemaker, intercepted by sitting up and offering her outstretched arm for Suleiman to climb. "You are our tutor and friend. First we pray to Allah, the gracious, and then we will go with much speed to break our fast."

Ara muttered under her breath as she stared at the ceiling with ill grace, then stared in shock, suddenly awake. "Found one!" There on the ceiling was a double reflection symmetry. This one was blue and gold with umber edges. But it was complete, not flawed in any way.

Layla leaned her head back to see. "It's always dark when we are here. The symmetries are all around us and we have never noticed."

"Good, you found it," Suleiman said, sounding impatient. "We now know that you can identify it. Now hurry, we must eat!"

Chapter 24

It was a day among days: the sunlight was brilliant, a gentle breeze blew, and all seemed right in the world. Suleiman, full of mouse energy, took an interest in all their activities. Perhaps too much so, thought Ara, still miffed with the mouse. Zoriah had taken pity on them and, handing them a basket of food, shooed them out into the gardens.

Celebrating their release from work, the girls walked through the gardens, floated leaves down the many streamlets and chased each other around the trees. A tiny reprieve from the strain of the past weeks.

Ara found one more symmetry while dallying in the Garden of the Lindaraja and showed Layla the small row of green rosettes that had both horizontal and vertical symmetries. Suleiman, after anxiously scanning the sky for hawks, sat down under a lacy fern surrounded by four almonds, three pomegranate seeds and a hefty piece of bread scavenged from the basket. As the day dwindled, Ara and Layla felt again the pressure of time. They packed up their belongings and their mouse and headed back to the palace.

Fatima, Maryam, and Rabab were sitting in an enclosed garden embroidering when the girls walked by. Rabab, telling a story, held Fatima's rapt attention.

"I'm not one to gossip, but I know what I saw," Rabab said. "The wazir was talking at the Palace Gate to a couple of Infidels, and a more disreputable couple of men I have never seen. One of them, standing behind the other, had something wrong with his legs, poor man. Looked like he had two clubfeet. The other man had a plumed hat and a scowl on his face you wouldn't believe. I couldn't understand a word they said, what with the two of them waving their hands in the air and shouting in that strange barbaric language of theirs. The wazir looked angry too. He kept looking back at the palace as if in disbelief. I know the sultan told us to be polite to those people, but no good can come from running around with the People of the Book."

After a quick look at the girls, Maryam moved uncomfortably against the bench. "Aunt," she suggested, "let us speak of this another time."

But Rabab went on without missing a beat. "And that's not all. One of my friends has a brother, who was told by a very reliable source that he heard the wazir talking to a wall. I think he must have been drinking wine," she added knowingly. "And you know what the Prophet Muhammad, peace be upon Him, says about drinking. Well, she said that her brother's friend saw him with his very own eyes. Abd al-Rahmid was standing in front of a wall and talking to it. As if he were having a conversation, you understand."

"Aunt Rabab, the girls," Maryam attempted once again.

Fatima, who had been spellbound up to now, leaned forward. "Well, normally, I wouldn't mention a thing. Never say an unkind word, that's my way, you know. But I have a friend whose servant said that the wazir has developed a peculiar dislike of lizards. He pays the gypsy children to bring him lizards. No, not special lizards," she added at Rabab's raised eyebrows. "Just lizards. And you know what he does with the lizards? He steps on them and crushes their heads. Did you ever hear the like?"

Both women stopped in awe of each other's tale. Maryam bit her lip in annoyance, then said, "I saw the loveliest cinnamon and rose-colored silk produced here in Andalusia. I believe it's even nicer than the foreign made silk. Aunt, don't you think it would make a wonderful outfit for Layla? I was hoping that you would advise me on this; you have such a way with clothes."

Rabab blinked and gazed at her sister's daughter's child. "But lizards, why would anyone kill lizards?"

Ara and Layla stood stock-still, afraid to move. Neither girl looked at the other, somehow afraid they would give away their secret. Suleiman trembled in Ara's sleeve.

Maryam glanced at her daughter before saying firmly, "I think we should not concern ourselves in the affairs of the wazir. I'm sure there is a very reasonable explanation. Perhaps there is some misunderstanding. Someone must have misspoken." Her face was tight. "Ladies, I must take my leave of you now. I will accompany the girls back into the palace. You will excuse me." She stood and bowed before gathering her supplies. "Girls, may I join you?"

Layla responded with a start. "Of course, Mother. It would give us great pleasure."

Together they walked toward the Court of the Myrtles, no one speaking until Maryam's careful, "About the discussion you overheard. I would ask that you not repeat gossip. Fatima and Rabab are older and wise. I value their advice in many things. But," she said with a sigh, "they are not always as discreet as I would wish, and the walls have ears." She sighed again.

"Mother...I..." Layla started, "about the basket."

Ara almost tripped in her panic. "No," she hissed as quietly as she could.

"Yes, my daughter?" Maryam said.

Layla looked at the ground in discomfort before stammering. "I...I...could I get a pet?"

"Oh, yes, the basket," Maryam said with a smile. "Well, what kind of animal do you want? Perhaps Rabab would let you have one of her parakeets if we were to ask."

"No, I don't think I want a parakeet," Layla looked down at the ground. "I was just thinking about Aunt Rabab, though. She's a good person, isn't she? And even though sometimes she doesn't do everything quite right, we still love her, don't we?"

120

Maryam stopped in her tracks to look directly at her daughter. "Is there something wrong? Something you need to tell me?"

"No, I mean, at least not yet. It's kind of a surprise, and I can't tell you for a few weeks. But you know that I would never do anything bad, don't you?"

Maryam considered the girls for a long time, weighing her impressions of Layla's guilt and Ara's worry. "Girls, I trust you with my heart and my honor. My love is always there for you, no matter what. All I care about is that you are safe."

She thought for a moment, then asked, "Does it have to do with the basket?"

Two heads nodded.

"Does some dependable adult know about this secret?" Again the heads nodded.

She relaxed slightly. "Then I can wait. When you are ready, I would love to know your surprise."

I don't think so, thought Ara. Carefully, she stared at the ground.

The rest of the walk was made in silence. Maryam looked at the girls quizzically once or twice but seemed lost in her own concerns. They entered through the side of the Hall of the Lions and walked around the arched peristyles toward the Hall of the Two Sisters. Both girls were preoccupied with what had happened; Layla worried about deceiving her mother, and Ara focused on finding symmetries. At last Maryam spoke. "I must speak to my sister-wife, Thana. I'll see the two of you at our evening meal."

The girls hurried into the Hall of the Two Sisters. Ara peered around behind one wall-hanging after another. When she pulled back the tapestry next to the arched doorway, she gasped. A huge crack stretched from floor to ceiling. The Alhambra was failing, being destroyed at its very core. She ran her fingers over the break as if she could hold it together, but nothing happened.

In the space near her hand, a double symmetry tile with a gold leaf on red graced the arched doorway with a slightly out-of-position leaf. As she looked, that tile righted itself, as if suddenly aware that it had gotten out of position with its fellow tiles. From a distance, lions roared. The crack narrowed. A mere second later, she stumbled, yelping in surprise at the ungainly weight hanging from her sleeve.

Layla looked to see Ara struggling with a large cat. "Oh, no, it's trying to get Suleiman," she yelled and ran to the rescue.

"Shhh," Ara told her. "Someone might hear." She and the scruffy tabby, which clung desperately to her sleeve, fell in an unceremonious heap to the floor.

With a disgusted look at Layla, the cat commented, "Thank you for your concern, but I have no interest in eating mice." Suleiman rearranged himself into a more dignified position and took stock of his new form. After he'd convinced himself that all was in good order, he began a careful grooming, muttering over every misplaced hair. Layla helped Ara off the floor. They both stared at the cat.

"Did you have to knock me down?" Ara stomped her foot in exasperation. "Can't you warn me when you're changing?"

The cat barely glanced up from his grooming. "You're the one who saw the symmetry. Don't blame me for your poor planning."

Layla planted herself between the feuding friends. "What are we going to tell Mother?"

Ara grinned. "Well, you said you wanted a pet."

Layla could visualize her mother's look of disbelief. "Your pardon, Suleiman, but I don't think Mother would believe me."

"Your pardon, Layla," he retorted, not bothering to look up this time. "But I'm not interested in being anyone's pet."

"At least we found the symmetry long before the time limit. It wasn't as hard as we thought it would be," Ara said, bouncing up and down on her toes.

Layla continued to look skeptically at the cat. "But how do we keep him with us? We can't carry him in a basket. He's... well...fat."

Suleiman turned his back on the girls and continued grooming. "Size is important. No one likes a scrawny cat. I am ample and substantive, not fat," he hissed over his shoulder.

Ara smiled hopefully at him. "Come on, Suleiman, we have to go." Suleiman ignored her.

"Here, kitty, kitty," Layla called. She pulled out a piece of fish from their luncheon basket and waved it in the air.

"Don't do that," he implored, sniffing the air.

"Let's go. I think he'll follow us now," Layla whispered to Ara, and she continued to wave the fish in the air.

They exited the Hall of the Two Sisters, two girls and a large reluctant tabby. As they passed the fountain, Ara glanced over. She stopped short.

"Layla! My lion is missing."

Chapter 25

Tahirah slowly came out of her meditation. The healing continued, so the double symmetries must have been found. Sooner than required, she reflected with some pride.

Her skin prickled as she felt a magical presence enter her room. Surprised and startled, she sought to focus her senses back to the physical world. Somehow, her mathemagic wards had not prevented something from entering. She had thought herself safe, but her protections and defenses had not held. She opened her eyes and looked slowly around the room, prepared for the worst.

A fierce lion sat before her in full feline fury. "You are back," he said, watching with eyes that saw all. "The cubs need protecting. They are young and clawless."

Tahirah blinked in surprise and delight. "Oh, noble one, I am honored by your presence. Why have you come?"

Light danced through the lion; his image wavered as he spoke. "We have been bespelled by one who betrays and tortures the Red Palace. Circle upon circle of spells bound us, and now one more band has been broken. He has harmed what is ours to protect. Loyalty shadows him now, Vigilance and Justice close behind. We cannot fulfill our duty until all the spells are undone. Meanwhile, we watch and wait." His eyes glowed, and the tip of his tail thrashed.

"Why do you come to me?"

"Our cubs, you watch over them." The lion began to pace.

"Ara and Layla?" Tahirah smiled to herself at the thought of the girls as cubs.

"Yes, the cubs of the harem. They are freeing the bindings on us. We protect our own."

Tahirah carefully phrased her next question, afraid to offend the proud cat. "I called you and you did not answer. Might I know your name that I might call you in need?'

"My name?" He looked away uncomfortably before growling. "It is unimportant. You might call one of my brothers, Patience or Endurance."

Tahirah hesitated, then asked, "Do all twelve have names?"

The lion lifted his massive shoulders in an almost human shrug. "Yes, the ones I mentioned and, of course, Strength and Prudence. But this is not the time for a family history. My brothers and I were bound in deep dream by the wazir's spell. Now we are awake and can watch the evil one."

"You plan on harming the wazir?" Tahirah asked, troubled.

"His death is fated. Payment is due; there is no other pathway open to him. He has chosen his way and walks it as we speak," the cat snarled.

Tahirah looked off and away. "I would hope that you would be merciful."

"We are merciful. He will not suffer long." The lion's eyes glittered with an inner tension. "But you must hurry. Danger approaches."

Tahirah stood up, a chilling fear suddenly upon her. "What kind of danger?"

"The evil one, the wazir, hunts the cubs, just as we hunt him." The lion stood at the door and abruptly disappeared; tawny lights sparkled in his wake.

Chapter 26

The room was silent but for the trickling water from the fountain. As if a tooth had been pulled, only a gap remained where the lion had been. Layla stood, awestruck. "What do you think happened?"

Ara studied the fountain, unable to make sense of it. "He can't be gone," she said, her voice cracking. "He's my favorite."

"Maybe he's being repaired?" Layla offered doubtfully. The two girls circled the area, finding no clues as to the missing lion.

"Should we tell someone?" Ara questioned, unsure if her lion missing was good or bad.

"Yes, let's find my mother."

The girls edged into the King's Hall hand in hand with Suleiman trailing after, all his attention on the fish in Layla's basket.

The wazir strode purposefully across the room. "So, daughters of the harem, here you are. I would speak with you."

Suleiman backed up, spitting, his tail puffed out like a feather duster. Ara was unable to force a word out.

"Perhaps some other time, Abd al-Rahmid," came a slightly breathless voice from across the room. Tahirah rapidly entered, her white cloak fluttering behind her. "They're late as it is for their class." She flashed her hand across his path and a burst of stars danced in rapid succession across the stone floor forming a line—Tahirah and the girls on one side; the wazir on the other. If Ara ever doubted that Tahirah was a powerful mathemagician, she believed now.

The wazir hesitated for a second as though confused, then forced a false smile. "Tahirah, how nice to see you," he said, eyes narrowed with dislike. Then his voice took on the authority of his office. "But, I must insist on speaking with these two."

Ara felt the blood drain from her face. Tahirah came up beside her, and another coil of stars spun about at a twist of her hand. "It's late. You need to go about the sultan's business, don't you?" She turned her back to the wazir and, with a conspiratorial wink, said to the girls, "Come along."

He shook his head as if trying to clear it, then touched the wall. Ara saw the tile writhe beneath his hand. Then the wazir drew in a breath and seemed to gather strength. "Now," he said. "I need to speak to them now."

Tahirah smiled serenely as she steered the girls out of the room. "Regrettably, not today. We are behind in our lessons."

The wazir started forward as if to push Tahirah aside when a low hiss stopped him in his tracks. Looking around in surprise, his eyes fixed on Suleiman, whose every hair stood on end as he backed slowly away from the wazir. "A cat," Abd al-Rahmid said contemplatively. "A portly cat with the glow of magic surrounding him." A sly look of comprehension crossed his face.

Tahirah opened her mouth as if to speak, but instead she flicked her hand once again. Out spilled tiny diamonds that shimmered in the air. They settled lightly on each of the girls' feet then blinked out of sight. The wazir looked around as if uncertain, and Ara thought they might all succeed in escaping.

Suleiman made a sudden leap for the doorway and freedom. The wazir jerked as if the magic had suddenly released. He rushed after Suleiman but halted abruptly as a lion, as transparent as if formed of mist or smoke, materialized in his way. "Your destiny awaits," the lion said.

Abd al-Rahmid hesitated for a brief white-knuckled second before stepping through the bodiless lion. "Go back to your fountain," he jeered. "You can do me no harm." He dashed after Suleiman into the gardens.

The lion image wavered, then disappeared. A wisp of golden motes of light remained where he had stood.

After a moment of stunned silence, the girls exploded with a whirlwind of words, the loudest being Ara's, "My lion, that was my lion!"

"The wazir knows! What are we to do? What about Suleiman?"

A visibly shaken Tahirah quieted them with a gesture. "We must leave. The wazir could come back at any second. Suleiman knows enough to go to my quarters. Come, we must hurry."

"But what if Suleiman gets caught?" Ara whispered, afraid for her friend. Their petty bickering was now a thing of the past.

"The stone lion bought him time. Cats are quick and wary. Suleiman should be safe," Tahirah said.

Ara wished she could believe there was more to those words than just hope.

"We will speak no more of this until we are within the protection of my chambers."

Chapter 27

Tahirah's hand shook slightly, belying the calm of her face as she poured cups of lemon tea and passed one to each of the girls.

Ara looked around as if unsure what had happened, while Layla stared pensively at the empty basket.

After a long sip of the tea, Tahirah leaned back against the cushions with a slow sigh. "I was afraid I was too late," she confessed. "The stone lion came to warn me, but I was dazed from my trance and then bemused that a lion had come to me. I was so afraid that my tardiness would cost your safety." There was quiet in the room as all contemplated the danger the wazir posed.

"He can't come in here, can he?" Layla looked anxiously at the door.

Tahirah reached across and stroked her hair, "No, my child. We are safe here. No evil can pass my door. And he *is* evil," she added with a slight shudder. "We need to finish finding all the symmetries as quickly as possible. He doesn't yet connect you with the magic. He sees you as children and powerless. I cast a spell of forgetfulness on all of us in the doorway. Unfortunately, that spell only works for humans. Suleiman, I couldn't protect.

"We need more time," she said, almost to herself, then to the girls, "It would be best if you could stay within the harem as much as possible. Don't give the wazir cause to remember. Avoid his presence. He can't go into the harem, nor can he harm you there. If we are lucky, his recollection of us will seem as a scattered dream. He will have trouble discerning fact from a distant flight of his imagination. Unfortunately," she added, frowning, "he will remember Suleiman, and now he knows that Suleiman has transformed."

Layla moved to sit closer to Tahirah. "I'm frightened."

"Me too," Ara agreed.

Tahirah closed her eyes and leaned her head against the wall before saying, "You are wise to be. I was lulled into a false sense of safety, and that is now over." She placed her hand across her brow as if warding off a headache. "How much time do we have before the next change must take place—about three days?"

Both girls nodded, then jumped as two paws appeared at the window. Claws scrabbled for purchase on the outside wall as Suleiman painfully pulled himself up to the window ledge and squeezed through the lattice grating.

Ara and Layla rushed to his side, helping him from the sill. "We're so happy to see you." Ara cuddled him in her arms. "I didn't mean all the things I said."

Embarrassed and pleased by the display of affection, he started to purr. Tahirah looked away, wiping a tear of relief from her face.

Ara sat down with the purring cat in her lap. Layla opened the basket and pulled out some fish, which Suleiman ate daintily from her hand.

Tahirah smiled at the group. "Suleiman, we rejoice in your escape and are grateful that you were able to join us so quickly. How did you get away?"

The cat stopped purring. "I hid behind a drainpipe right outside the door. The wazir sped past in his hurry to catch up with me. In my wisdom, I crouched in the shadows beneath a small spiny bush, while he searched the gardens. Soon he continued west beyond the fig trees. When I no longer heard him, I crept between the roses and into the trees beyond."

Ara and Layla petted Suleiman, praising his stealth and skill, and he purred again.

"We must focus on our next lesson. Fortunately, it is a simple one." Tahirah went over to the collection of tiles, sorting through until she picked out four. "Band symmetry are objects that have symmetry along a band or row, correct?" she asked.

"Yes," the girls chorused.

Tahirah moved the tiles in front of them.

"The simplest symmetry is called a translation. The design or object moves one space across the row. It does not reflect. It looks different upside down and right side up, so there is neither horizontal nor vertical symmetry. In fact, it is unchanged in every way but for the fact that it is moved along the row one space. Note that you can tell it's not reflected because the flower stem points in one direction only. If it reflected vertically, the stem would alternate pointing to the left and to the right."

"But that's boring," Ara said, baffled, looking at the simple flower buds. "How can that be anything? It's too easy."

Tahirah smiled. "Not quite as easy as it may seem. Here, look at this one." She pulled out six other tiles.

"It's a double reflection—wait," Ara frowned. "It isn't."

"That right, it isn't. Now explain why."

Layla peered over her shoulder as Ara frowned at the tiles. "Well, the red line that goes up the middle—it isn't the same on both sides. It doesn't reflect. In fact," Ara said, looking at it critically, "it doesn't reflect horizontally either. But that's strange. It almost does."

Tahirah settled in a bit more. "Good, you see the difference. Symmetry must obey rules, and this one does not follow those rules for reflection. This is a simple translation. Another word for this symmetry's motion is slide."

"Oh," Layla said, showing more interest, "a slide, like in dance, a stepping to the side?"

Tahirah laughed. "Yes, very much like dance. The only way this symmetry group can move is by stepping to the side." She looked out the window. "It is nearing dark. I'll walk you into the harem where you will be safe. The wazir cannot go there, nor can any man. Remember, be careful. I've done what I can to confuse the wazir. Keep Suleiman away from him, but most important, do not put yourselves in danger."

Chapter 28

Sleep didn't come easily to the girls that night. Ara wanted to go back to the fountain to attempt a conversation with her lion. Maybe now he would show himself to her and speak. Layla, terrified of the wazir, argued long and hard that if the lion wanted to talk to them, he knew where they were. Suleiman, after thoroughly investigating the room, selected a soft pillow and, purring blissfully, kneaded it with his front paws before falling asleep.

"Girls, it is almost dawn and soon time for prayers. Why are you not up and about?" To Ara, lost in restless sleep, Su'ah's voice seemed far away. Something soft flecked across her nose. She opened her eyes slightly.

The tail swept across her face again. "Achoo," she sneezed. Suleiman pushed the covers up a bit to poke his nose outside the blanket. He'd crawled under last night complaining of a draft.

"Are you coming down with a cold?" Su'ah asked.

Ara shoved Suleiman back under the covers. "No, something just tickled my nose. I'm fine."

Su'ah stood gazing out the window at the brightening sky. "Looks like another beautiful morning." She stood watching for a moment, and then said. "Why, there's the wazir. What's he doing?"

Ara jumped up and ran to the window to look through the honeycombed slats. "Where?" she breathed, leaning against the sill. Layla opened her eyes wide.

Su'ah pointed to a shadowy figure standing backlit by a flickering torchlight from the palace. "See, it's him all right. What's he doing with that cat?"

The sun peeked its head over the horizon illuminating the scene: a tortoise-shell cat crouched in a corner, spitting furiously.

The wazir, looking disgusted, kicked at it, but it darted between his legs, escaping as the voice of the muezzin rang out. The call to prayer. The wazir slammed his fist against the wall and then hurried away. Ara and Layla quickly got their prayer rugs and, facing Mecca, began to pray.

Praise be to God, Lord of the worlds!
The compassionate, the merciful!
King on the day of reckoning!
Thee only do we worship, and to Thee do we cry for help.
Guide Thou us on the straight path,
The path of those to whom Thou hast been gracious; with
Whom thou art not angry, and who go not astray.

Beneath the tousled bedcovers, Ara could hear Suleiman perform his devotions.

Washed and scrubbed from their baths, the girls returned to their sleeping quarters. Su'ah had left earlier to watch over Dananir's small son. Layla went directly to the bed, wanting to collect Suleiman before they left for breakfast.

"He's gone," Layla whispered. Panic lurked in her voice.

"He can't have disappeared." Ara grabbed the covers, looked under them, and then started searching the room. "He knows we need him to be with us when he changes, and twelve hours have already gone by. He's a very smart cat. Or, at least, he was a smart tutor," she amended.

Layla ran to the window to scan the yard below. "Where could he be?"

"I'm here," Suleiman announced, slinking into the room. The fur on his neck stood out.

Layla rushed over to him and cradled him in her arms. "Where did you go? We were worried."

Suleiman shivered. "I went to speak with the Lions, feline to feline. We have much in common. They are magical lions, and I am a cat transformed through magic. I hoped they might tell me how to break this spell faster."

"What happened?" Layla asked. "Didn't they help?"

He wriggled, wanting to get down. "The power they hold is overwhelming. Being near them is like staring at the sun too long. Even partially bound by the wazir's magic, they radiate; they pulse with power. They knew, of course, that I had been transformed." He leapt to the floor and paced restlessly.

"They criticized me for wanting to change back to my human self. Me, a Turk of the tribe of Qizilbash! The lions, Wisdom and Reason, said I should take the opportunity to learn from each transformation. I was too prideful, they said." He flashed the girls a look before twitching his tail in indignation.

Neither girl spoke, uncertain what to say. Suleiman continued pacing. Both recalled him in his human form: smart, competent but very pompous.

"What are you supposed to learn?" Ara asked.

"They said that I was wasting valuable magic by not using the time wisely. That each animal shape I turn into had lessons to teach. They were not sympathetic." He bristled.

Suleiman continued to pace while the girls snuck quick looks at each other.

"Did they hint at what they thought you should learn?"

"Humility," Suleiman spat. "I believe that was the first lesson."

Ara winced. Layla considered that for a moment, then said, "What about sympathy for those who are powerless?"

"What about it?" the cat snapped.

"That was something you learned as a lizard. Maybe that's what they meant."

Ara looked at her cousin in amazement.

Suleiman's tail flicked in annoyance, and Ara thought he was going to dismiss Layla's suggestion. He reached up to the weaving hanging on the loom and sharpened his claws. "Perhaps that's true. Maybe the lions are right. There is something to learn here. I need to think on this."

"Please, could you think about it without destroying Su'ah's weaving?" Ara implored.

"Your pardon," he apologized, self-consciously removing his claws from the material. "I need to go for a walk and consider Wisdom's words."

"But we need you here!" Ara protested. "You need to help us find the translation symmetry." The cat stared at her and flattened his ears. Ara grasped at a thought. "Was Wisdom my lion's name? Was he the one you spoke to?"

"Your lion didn't stoop to introducing himself," Suleiman huffed. "Yes, a walk is just what I need."

"You can't leave. It's not safe," Layla said reasonably.

Suleiman gave her a look that would curdle milk. "I'm a cat—I come and go as I please. I escaped through cunning yesterday—I can do it again." He arched his back in what seemed a casual stretch before trotting toward the door. "Don't worry, you won't have trouble finding translation symmetries. There are too many to count in the Alhambra," he said dismissively. "If I see the broken one, I'll let you know."

And he was gone.

Ara was the first to recover. "I might guess *his* lesson is independence," she said.

"Now what?" Layla asked.

Ara picked up her lute and headed for the door. "We have classes to attend. I guess we continue on. We have until three hours before sunset the day after tomorrow to find this symmetry. We must wait for his return, otherwise we won't know what he changes into."

After an unhappy look at the door, Layla grabbed her dance clothes and calligraphy stylus and followed Ara.

Neither could look at the other. Unspoken was the fear—what if he never returned?

Chapter 29

By early the next morning both girls were beside themselves with worry. Suleiman had not returned, and only a few handfuls of hours remained. Ara had found a translation right outside their room. But it was whole, not broken.

"Look what I found at the fishpond." Su'ah walked in the room with a large gray tabby curled across her thin arms. Jada trailed along behind her. "I'm sure he must belong to someone. He came right up to me and purred."

Ara thought she would faint from relief.

Su'ah sat down and continued petting the cat. "I saw mouse droppings on the floor a few days ago. This will solve the problem. He looks like a good mouser."

Suleiman gave them a don't-get-me-started look. Ara snorted, trying to hide her laughter while Layla rushed to Su'ah's side exclaiming, "He's wonderful," to both Suleiman's and Su'ah's delight.

"I thought you might like a cat, Layla. Your mother said you wanted a pet." Su'ah scratched Suleiman under the chin, and his eyes glazed over with pleasure. "I knew you wouldn't want one of those noisy parakeets that the Infidels brought Rabab. They flit all over the place, never sitting still for a moment."

The purring stopped, and Suleiman was immobile. A glint of light came from a slit in his eyes, and abruptly it disappeared.

"I'll call him Hannibal—he looks like a good, quiet cat. Here Layla, you want to hold him? Sit down here, and I'll set him in your lap. Jada, you sit next to her, and no pulling his tail again!"

Ara, now doubled over in hysterics, was having a hard time watching the two former adversaries snuggle. But after all their past disagreements when both were slaves and human, Suleiman now, in his cat form, seemed quite pleased by the affection, however misplaced.

Su'ah placed him in Layla's lap where he continued to purr. "Ara, what *are* you carrying on about over there? I see nothing funny," Su'ah said with some indignation. "Well, maybe he is a little heavy," Su'ah conceded, looking at the cat with a calculating eye. "Someone must have been overfeeding him. He'll slim down quick enough when he has to forage on his own."

Suleiman glared at Su'ah, his tail twitching.

"Have you ever seen a cat so smart looking. Why, I'd almost believe he can understand me." Suleiman glared at her, his tail twitching. "Layla, you must be petting him too hard, he doesn't seem to like that."

Suleiman dropped into a quick catnap, and pleased that her mouser was settling in so nicely, Su'ah left to take Jada back to her mother.

Ara shook the cat awake as soon as she was gone. "Where were you? We were worried."

Miffed at the rude awakening, Suleiman snarled and made a perfunctory swipe in her direction. "I was out thinking. The lions have a point." He yawned and stretched. "There are important lessons to learn."

Ara waved his comment away. "But our time is almost over. We have only two more hours. We needed you here."

"Well, yes," he agreed acidly on his way to the door, "in a perfect world I would sit beside you and wait on your pleasure. But I have one more important task to do. I'll be back in plenty of time." Before she could grab him, he streaked out of the room.

Chapter 30

Ara once again found herself looking out the window. At least Layla had found the broken symmetry and promptly covered it with a tapestry so Ara wouldn't see it and risk another transformation until Suleiman returned.

But time was running out. Only minutes remained.

Allah take that cat!

Thump, thump, thump—Suleiman bounded into the room. "Hide me quick, they're after me." They heard footsteps pound up the stairs.

Fear streaked across Layla's face. "Is it the wazir?"

"No, worse! Rabab and Zoriah," Suleiman spat, racing around the room, looking for a hiding place. "Hurry, they're almost here."

The girls looked to one another and realized what they needed to do. Layla ran to the tapestry and flipped it up. As Ara gazed at the symmetry, it rapidly realigned itself. She felt a tingling throughout her body as the Alhambra healed. Deep within the walls she heard lions, many lions, roaring.

Zoriah rushed in, a gasping, limping Rabab not far behind. "Have you seen a cat?" Zoriah demanded, looking around the room. There on the rug sat a dog, leisurely scratching his ear.

"Where did *that* come from?" Rabab wheezed, pointing. She said down on the bed, panting from exertion.

Zoriah, momentarily distracted, stared at the tan and white hound. "*That* can't stay in your sleeping rooms. Whose is it?"

Ara walked over and wrapped her arms around him. "He just appeared. Please don't make me put him outside." The dog perked up his long pointy ears and, wagging his tail, gave her a sloppy lick on the face.

Zoriah winced.

Rabab recoiled at the sight. "Mohammed tells us dogs are dirty."

Ara held up the dog's long ears. "But not salukis. They are hunting dogs, favored by Mohammed."

"We'll discuss this in a minute." Zoriah looked at the girls suspiciously. "Have you seen a cat? Su'ah found a cat this morning, a gray cat."

Studiously avoiding looking at Suleiman, Ara said, "The cat ran out of here about an hour ago. We couldn't catch him."

Rabab, finally regaining her breath, burst out, "The horrible creature tried to eat my parakeets. I heard their squawks and ran into my room. There he was pinning one of my little birds against the cage with his paw. Once he saw me, the beast scuttled out the room. We followed him here."

Ara looked at the dog in disgust before responding with a slight edge to her voice, "Maybe he's gone now. You know how cats are independent. They never stay where they belong nor wait on anyone's pleasure but their own."

Suleiman's ears folded down.

The older woman bent awkwardly to check in the bedding. "You're sure he's not in here?"

"Rabab, there's a dog sitting over there." Zoriah's voice was dry. "Do you really think a dog would just be sitting there if a cat came into the room?"

Ara quietly thanked Allah that Layla had found the broken symmetry. She watched as Layla surreptitiously placed her foot on top of a lone yellow feather.

Rabab pushed herself upright. "That's true, of course. But I was sure I saw him head this way. Where else could he have gone?"

She looked around the room again, stopping at the dog that had found Layla's slipper and was chewing on it. "I don't think we should allow dogs in the harem—they're dirty."

Zoriah studied the dog one last time. "Ara, I'm going to have to talk to your father about that dog. You can't keep him in the harem. He looks flea-ridden, he's grimy—he could be vicious."

Suleiman stood and wagged his tail. Ara gave her a wistful, appealing smile. "You can see he's gentle. I'll give him a bath, and he won't be any trouble. Please, just for a few days." Ara gave her a wistful, appealing smile.

Layla crossed the room to join Ara. "Could we at least take him to see Tahirah? She loves animals."

Suleiman perked his ears and thumped his tail.

The thought of the immaculate Sufi cavorting with the hound was too much for Zoriah. "Somehow, although it seems beyond all possibility, it just might be so. Tahirah could be amused to see a dog."

Her expression fell. "But I'm afraid not. I saw her not an hour ago on her way into Granada. She had to go to the khanqa, the Sufi hospice. One of the Sufis there had taken a turn for the worse and needed her comfort. She's not expected back until after the evening meal. You can visit with her tomorrow."

Ara's eyes widened. "Tomorrow? But that's hours and hours away."

"Exactly," Zoriah agreed, focusing once again on the girls. "And you need to help us find that cat. Until Tahirah returns tomorrow, we will put the dog in the stables."

Rabab's brow wrinkled. "Where are all these animals coming from, anyway? First a cat, and now this dog. At least it seems friendly." She moved over to the door. "He probably belongs to someone. See how he looks...he's the fattest hound I've ever seen."

Zoriah shook her head. "Lately, nothing is going as it should. The wazir has been asking odd questions of all the servants. I don't understand."

Ara and Layla didn't move. Suleiman curled his tail between his legs.

Su'ah slowly ambled through the door and gave a start of surprise. "What's that dog doing here?" With a sour look, she returned to the door and called out, "Here, kitty, kitty."

"That cat almost ate my parakeets." Rabab glowered.

"Su'ah stood with her hand on the door. "That cat is going to rid us of vermin. That's much more important than any silly birds. Can't have mice running around all over the place. Hannibal! Here, kitty. Come, puss."

Layla walked over and placed a gentle hand on Su'ah's shoulder. "Though I believe that particular cat no longer values his independence, I'm not sure he will return."

Su'ah snorted. "Don't be ridiculous. Cats always come back. You know the expression, 'Feed a cat, own a cat.' I'll put out some goat milk for him. You'll see." She nodded sagely as she left in search of cat-pleasing liquids.

Rabab, her feathers still ruffled about her birds, sniffed. "What is the harem coming to? First that horrible cat, and now this flea-ridden hound."

Zoriah yanked a strand of her hair in exasperation. "We will help find the cat now." She gestured firmly toward the dog. "I'll deal with this situation later."

Rabab and Zoriah left the room, dragging the girls in reluctant tow in search of a missing gray tabby. The dog stayed behind closed doors, worrying a slipper.

Chapter 31

When the sun had barely begun its path across the sky the next morning, the girls raced to the Palace of the Partal where the Sufi stayed. Tahirah stood at its entrance, smiling at the sight of the hound trotting happily beside them. He waved a found stick around in delight.

"This is a splendid stick!" He dropped it in front of them. "You know, I wouldn't mind if you threw it." He waited expectantly. While both girls were pleased with this new and cheerier Suleiman, neither wanted to throw the now drool-covered thing. Suleiman finally grinned and grabbed it again. "Still, it's a great day and a wonderful stick."

He carried it high in the air, tossing his head in pleasure until he spied Tahirah. He dropped the stick. "There she is. I can't believe it. What a thrill." He raced full out toward her, leaping and dancing around her until, to his delight, she laughed out loud.

"I missed you so." He danced around in a circle once again and ran back to get the stick. "Did you see my stick? I found it on the way here. Isn't it a great stick?"

Tahirah reached for the stick and, after a short playful tussle with Suleiman, threw it with a practiced arm. Suleiman bounded after it. Ara and Layla hugged Tahirah, then stepped back when Suleiman returned with the stick.

Ara watched his antics with mixed emotions. "I've never seen Suleiman this happy." Under the circumstances, it didn't seem right that her stodgy tutor should be so lighthearted, even if he was magically transformed into a dog's body.

"It is wonderful, is it not?" Tahirah threw the stick again. "There's a lesson to be learned from dogs. Life is fleeting. Enjoy it to its fullest."

Layla nodded. "That's what the lions said."

Tahirah stopped. "You spoke to the lions?"

Suleiman returned again with his stick, dropped it at Tahirah's feet and panted. "No. I spoke to the lions. Or,"—he looked confused—"the cat did, anyway."

"I think we need to go into my rooms for a more private conversation." Tahirah said, then led the way. Servants nodded politely to them with only a few raised eyebrows at the hound trotting happily alongside.

A few moments later, enjoying tea and flaky delicacies, they lounged on the cushions. Suleiman stood at Tahirah's feet, catching pitched morsels of food.

"So, how did you come to speak to the lions?" she asked.

His ears went down, and he whined slightly, recalling his days as a cat. "I went to confer with them. They were disdainful of me." He thought a bit. "Of course, I too would be disdainful of a small cat were I a grand one. Perhaps that was the real problem."

Tahirah hid her smile. "Perhaps, but let's explore some other avenues of thought. Think back. What did the lions say to you?"

Suleiman sat down and scratched his ear before looking hopefully at her plate. "I told Ara and Layla already." He glanced at Tahirah. "I would remember better if you gave me one more of those little pastries."

She smiled understandingly, but replied in an uncompromising tone. "No blackmail, thank you very much. If you don't choose to tell me, the girls will be happy to do so. I wanted to give you the chance to tell your story yourself."

Suleiman's hung his head. "I'm sorry. You're my pack. Of course I'll tell you. I don't really need the treats." He turned his head slightly from the dish of pastries, drool dripping down his jaws.

Tahirah sighed and shook her head before tossing him a treat. "Suleiman, here, have a pastry. I can't stand to watch a grown dog drool."

It disappeared in a snap of jaws, and with a muffled *bismillah*, Suleiman gulped it down. "The lions were miffed at the cat. Discipline and Reason growled at him."

"You mean *YOU*," Ara interrupted. "You were the cat."

"Perhaps in the strictest sense, that may have been true," he conceded, getting up to circle uncomfortably. "Anyway, they, the lions, wanted me to use my enchanted time better. To learn and understand from each transformation."

"And are you?" Tahirah questioned.

He sat down and studied his paws. "As a lizard, I learned how it feels to be powerless; as a snake, I relearned the value of life. In mouse form, I understood that size does not define spirit." He whined again before speaking. "The cat learned that not all things can be done alone." He wagged his tail and perked up his ears. "But dogs, dogs are great. I can see this. Allah has, in his ultimate wisdom, given us the best traits."

"Which are..." Tahirah encouraged.

"Isn't it obvious? We're loyal to our pack and brave and joyous. A true companion. Best at work, best at—"

"Best at modesty," Ara said wryly, "most humble, most..."

"You are picking on me." Suleiman tucked his tail under his rump, his ears drooping once again. "Don't you like me anymore?"

Instantly ashamed, Ara leaned over and patted him on the head. "You are perfect. Whatever shape you take, I love you. I'm sorry. Everything seems to be happening too fast. I'm hiding things from Father, and I'm scared."

Suleiman grinned and gave her a couple of quick, understanding licks.

Tahirah reached out and put her arm around both friends. "Speaking of which, we need to do the next lesson. Suleiman, would you like to teach this one? I think rotation would be best."

He barked twice, then looked chagrined. "Sorry, when you speak many languages, it's hard not to fall into careless habits. Actually, I *would* like to explain rotation." He looked around for an example, and in turning, discovered to his wonder, his tail. He continued circling, trying to grab it. "See, here is a perfect example."

The girls saw nothing but a silly hound chasing his tail. "Perfect example of what?" Layla asked.

He continued the pursuit, making an occasional half-hearted grab for it. "Rotation. I'm turning around. It's obvious."

Ara turned a cartwheel while Layla did a pirouette. "You mean like that?"

Grinning, he sat. "Yes, but now you have to look at it in slow motion to see how it's different from a vertical reflection. Tahirah, would you pull out the tiles again?"

She patiently drew out four tiles and placed them before the dog. Suleiman placed a paw on the first tile. "Each of these is identical, like a translation, right?"

"Yes, " Ara agreed, "just as before."

Suleiman wagged his tail and woofed. "But now we will create rotations. We take the first one and place it so." He nudged two tiles into place. "See how with the first tile, the blue part of the design is on the top? And then how the second is turned one hundred eighty degrees? It is rotated." He placed a paw dead center between the two tiles. "With rotation, you pretend there is a point or hub in the center around which the object moves. Now you try it."

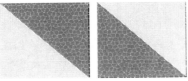

Ara looked at the tiles with interest. This was a lot like a game! She turned the next tile one hundred eighty degrees and placed it beside the first two.

Suleiman lay down beside them. "Pretend that you're holding your paw—sorry, I mean finger—in the middle. An immovable point. That point, at your finger, must stay in place as you turn the tile around."

"This is the third of the four motions," Tahirah said, joining in. "Reflection—which we also call a flip—translation or slide; and now rotation," she finished, having ticked them off on her fingers. "One of the remarkable things about rotation is that the double reflections also rotate."

Ara looked up. "Because it looks the same upside down and right side up?"

"Exactly. It includes a one hundred eighty degree rotation in the design, so it looks the same upside down or right side up." Tahirah turned both tiles upside down and then back again.

The dog woofed. "You forgot to mention that there _cannot_ be a flip in a rotation."

The mathemagician smiled, patting his head in agreement. "That is correct. For it to be considered rotation, it can't have a mirror in the design. It does not reflect. If it did, it could be a double reflection or possibly the seventh band symmetry which you have not yet learned."

Layla asked. "Could we see another example?"

"Take these same tiles and make another rotational symmetry," Tahirah suggested.

Uncertain, Layla picked up a tile. "How do you start?"

Suleiman woofed encouragingly before stuffing his nose under her arm. "You can do this. Look at all you've learned so far. Try."

She placed the first piece with the blue part facing down. The next tile she lined up exactly the same, then turned it one hundred eighty degrees to the right. Encouraged, she took the third piece and, placing it the same way as the original tile, rotated it one hundred eighty degrees yet again. The last tile she turned one hundred eighty degrees until the design cartwheeled across the floor.

Suleiman barked in glee and ran around the room. "See, you did it!"

Layla grinned. "I guess I did."

Everyone jumped at the knock on the door. Tahirah called out permission to enter. Her servant did so, then, bowing near to the floor, handed her a card on a silver tray. After dismissing her, Tahirah read the card. "The sultan requests the presence of his daughter and niece immediately in the Hall of the Kings. He wishes the dog to be brought before him."

She looked at the children, her eyes dark with concern. "It seems the owner of the dog has come forward."

Chapter 32

Ara sputtered, "But he can't have an owner. It's Suleiman." And then more thoughtfully, "This must be serious. The wazir must know it's Suleiman in dog form."

Layla sat in a daze, stunned that she was being hauled before her uncle.

Suleiman circled in the corner, whining—his ears pinned to his head and tail tucked despondently.

Three guards awaited them outside Tahirah's rooms. Tahirah positioned herself between the men and the girls, politely but firmly refusing to allow the girls to be taken to the Palace Court without her. No rope was permitted on Suleiman no matter how the guard argued. Finally, the guards agreed to wait outside while the group prepared to set off for the Hall of the Ambassadors. As they rounded up scarves, caftans and shoes, Tahirah assessed the situation. "Yes, I sense the hand of the wazir in this. He can't be certain, nor can he prove it without divulging what he has done. We know that Suleiman doesn't have an owner. Let us go prepared to deal with the worst possible likelihood, though perchance it is but a misunderstanding, *inshallah*."

Grabbing her caftan and trying to tidy herself up quickly, Ara muttered, "I hope that this is only Zoriah upset about finding a dog in her spotless rooms."

Tahirah looked over in sympathy at Ara. "I also wish this is so, but the note said the owner of the dog was there. Someone thinks—or wants the sultan to think—we have his dog."

She captured and held each girl's gaze. "You two must show your best side. We shall proceed carefully until we know what this is about. Whatever happens, be exceedingly polite and respectful. The sultan is in an awkward position. You know how much he loves you," she reminded them, "but as sultan, he cannot be seen to support his daughter and niece over another of his subjects. I will do as much as I can to help, but you must be seen as gracious and cooperative."

Ara's eyes brimmed with tears. "He does love me, doesn't he? Even though I spilled the dye in the Court of the Lions? He's not spoken to me since. I know I do things I ought not, but..."

Tahirah rushed over and held her close. "He loves you very, very much. You know this is true. You can demonstrate *your* love by making him proud of his daughter and by trusting him." She gently smoothed Ara's hair and smiled encouragingly at Layla.

Ara wiped away her tears and rubbed her nose. "I can do this. I *am* a sultan's daughter."

Tahirah nodded. "Remember, head high, and keep on the lookout for rotational symmetries; time is not our friend."

When they stepped out into the gardens, the impassive guards again moved to grab the dog, but Tahirah stopped them with a look and a few firmly spoken words. Layla, to everyone's surprise, sauntered along whistling while they walked. The guards, stiffly proper, kept glancing nervously at her until one of them finally broke into a grin.

Tahirah laughed. Suleiman got caught up in the pleasure of the melody and, untucking his tail, pranced alongside.

Ara grinned at her cousin before joining in with a bouncy harmony.

Tahirah laughed again. "That's a strange tune for you to know. How did you learn a gypsy song in the palace?"

Layla blushed at the attention. "I heard two servants singing it last month in the kitchen. I thought it might cheer me up, and it did."

Tahirah looked at their little group. "I think it cheered up all of us."

At the doorway to the Palace of the Myrtles, they hesitated and smiled assurances at one another before proceeding into the Hall of the Ambassadors. At the far end sat the sultan, grim-faced. Few people were there, but three veiled women in hijabs sat anxiously on side benches. Layla saw her father standing quietly to the side. She gasped upon recognizing the man talking to him

151

but quickly recaptured her mask of poise. Two advisors stood at the sultan's side cloaked in brown caftans, perplexed at the uproar over one dog.

The wazir, who stood before Layla's father, was obviously retelling his tale, waving his hands as he spoke. He turned as their feet tapped across the stone floor. "That's my dog," he said loudly. "That's my newly-purchased dog."

The sultan's jaw clenched. "Abd al-Rahmid, sit down, please. We will conduct this as a fair and objective discussion. All will be questioned and, by Allah's hand, the truth will be known."

The wazir made a motion toward the girls but checked himself as the guards tensed and reached for their swords. He stood rigidly in place, assessing the situation.

The sultan watched, his eyebrows pulled down in a frown. "Sit, I said."

Eyes still on the dog, the wazir bent and folded his legs beneath him.

Satisfied with his advisor's compliance, the sultan addressed his daughter and company. "Thank you for coming so quickly. A matter has been brought to my attention. A matter of a dog. An almost inconsequential thing, some might say." He looked at the wazir and shook his head. "But it has been addressed to our royal self to resolve. So it will be done, *inshallah*."

Ara bowed low. "We are your loyal subjects and strive to assist as we may."

A look of pride flashed across her father's face, then was gone. "We will begin. Abd al-Rahmid states that he recently purchased a dog."

"A dog for hunting, *shaykh*," the wazir interrupted. "Purchased at great cost."

"At great cost," the sultan repeated, briefly closing his eyes. "This morning, it was made known to me that a dog was found in the harem. My head advisor"—he gestured at the scowling man at his side—"stated he had lost such a dog. We now need to discover whose dog this is."

The wazir pointed a finger at Suleiman. "That is my dog. I would know him anywhere. I have great need of him, for we are to go hunting tomorrow."

The room stirred at the unseemliness of yet another outburst. Layla's father kept his face carefully neutral, though his hand seemed to twitch nearer to his sword. The other advisors looked perplexed. It was only a dog after all, and Allah did not favor them.

"Abd al-Rahmid, do you have proof that it belongs to you? Has the person who sold it to you come forward, or any witnesses who can verify that it is yours?"

The wazir didn't answer, leaving the questions to hang in the air like sharpened knives. Tahirah could sense his desperation. His eyes shifted as he searched for an answer.

The race is on, she thought. He knows his magic is failing and time is running out. She raised her head, speaking quietly but firmly into the silence. "The dog was found by the girls while in the harem. Abd al-Rahmid could not have entered there, nor could any man. The dog appeared lost and uncared for. This I swear is true."

"She is but a woman, *shaykh*," the wazir sputtered. "Easily mistaken and easily misled." His voice rose yet again. "She's a Sufi and bends Allah's word to fit her own wishes."

Several people gasped. Tahirah stood quietly, serenely awaiting the sultan's next words.

The sultan's eyes were hard. "Enough. She is a Sufi and a person of honor. I will not hear this again. No more outbursts or you will be reprimanded by my own hand." His pronouncement reverberated in the great room.

"Ara." He said in a calmer tone, "I want you to think before you answer. Is it possible that this dog is the property of my wazir?"

She looked directly at her father. "No, it is not."

"Layla. What say you?"

She blanched but said earnestly. "*Shaykh*, it's not his dog."

The sultan leaned back in his throne. Beside him, the wazir ground his teeth.

"Though each of you report having had the dog such a short time," the sultan said after considering, "I would think that the dog would remember his owner. I suggest we let the wazir call to him."

The wazir walked to stand large and overbearing in the center of the room. Suleiman cowered behind Ara, leaning hard against her leg.

"Dog, come! You know your master. You *must* obey." His eyes bored into Suleiman's.

Although he did not move a paw, Suleiman whimpered and cowered all the more.

The wazir raised his voice. "Come, I say, or it will go hard for you."

Suleiman lifted his head and stared at the wazir, the source of all his pain and misery. His hackles raised while a low growl started in his throat. His teeth bared, and his body tensed for a fight. An echoing roar sounded, from where no one could tell.

The wazir flinched, and the girls gained heart. Tahirah blinked in surprise. No one else seemed to hear. Suleiman, emboldened by the backing of a pride of lions, stood firm and continued growling.

The sultan looked curiously at the wazir. "Interesting that you try to have a discussion with a dog. The animal seems not to like you." He shrugged. "Perhaps that is telling in itself. Still, he does not go to you."

He nodded to his daughter. "Ara, would you step across the room and call the dog."

Ara walked away from Suleiman at a steady clip. After an anxious moment, he bounded after her, and growled again at the wazir on his way.

Suleiman pressed himself against Ara. She bent down to pat him and was rewarded with a quick lick of affection.

Her father cocked his head. "It seems that it is unnecessary for you to call the dog. It obviously trusts you. But as the dog is, according to Abd al-Rahmid, newly purchased, this does not decide ownership. I need more time to think on this."

The wazir, sweat dotting his face, protested with a self-effacing smile. His hands clenched and unclenched. "*Shaykh*, you are right, but he should not be left in these women's possession. He looks to be vicious and could harm your daughter. He needs to be returned to my hand."

After a long, slow stare at the wazir, the sultan spoke. "I thank my advisor for helping me make this decision. The dog will be taken to a secure location and well treated, until I have thought further on this. It seems there is more here than meets the eye."

Ara clung to the trembling hound as the guards approached. Her father leaned slightly forward toward her as they drew near and quietly avowed, "Upon my honor, the dog will not be harmed. I will give you an answer as quickly as possible."

Tahirah stepped forward to comfort both girl and dog. As the guards tied a rope around Suleiman, she turned to face the sultan, her white woolen cloak hiding none of the tension in her body. "Guard him well, as you would your most trusted servant." Abruptly, she turned and left, as if afraid of having said too much. The two girls followed, taking backwards glances as Suleiman, surrounded by guards, was taken away.

The sultan sat pondering the interest of so many in one small, rather ugly hound long after all had left.

Chapter 33

Ara and Layla were both weeping by the time they returned to Tahirah's rooms. Tahirah closed the door firmly and wiped her own eyes before admonishing, "We must not waste time in tears. The solution is within your power. Find the symmetries quickly before the wazir can cause Suleiman harm. Turn your sorrow and anger into something useful."

Layla blew her nose before asking, a catch to her voice, "But Suleiman is locked in the tower. How are we going to get him out? What will happen if he changes shape while we aren't near?"

"It is in the hands of Allah, the Merciful." Tahirah closed her eyes in acceptance. "We must trust and strive onward, *inshallah*. The magic will not wait. Tomorrow, Suleiman will either have changed or he will be a dog forever." She looked full in Layla's eyes. "We have no other choice. Nor does Suleiman."

Ara straightened her back and sniffed loudly. "Where should we look first?"

Tahirah shook herself before waving her hand as though to brush away a bothersome fly. "The day moves forward, and here is as good a place to start as any. It would be good if you seek rotational symmetries, to make sure that you can identify it. I'm sure you and Layla can find at least one rotational symmetry here *if* you put aside your fears."

The mathemagician turned toward the door. "While you are searching, I will see where Suleiman is being held and check on his well-being. We don't know where the broken one is, but it is sure to be somewhere within the walls of the Alhambra.

Forty minutes went by in quiet concentration before Ara called out, "Got one. And I checked—there is no mirror in the design."

Tahirah returned with news within the hour. "Suleiman is being held in the Tower of the Myrtles and is guarded by two sentries outside his door. They have orders that no one shall enter without the sultan's word. I also placed formulas around the entrance." She allowed herself a smile. "Two lions lie between Suleiman and the door—protecting. None shall pass them this night.

"Suleiman seems very sad, but at least for now, he is safe." She sighed. "I wish I knew what the wazir is planning. I need to look further into this. You two should go back to the harem. You may be able to see Suleiman from a window in the Palace of the Myrtles. I'll call the guards and walk you back myself." When Ara told her of their earlier find, she gave an approving smile, but added, "You must find the broken rotational symmetry, quickly."

Ara could hear mournful howling as soon as she walked outside. It drifted on the wind and slapped her as a reproach.

"Poor Suleiman," Layla said as the howl rose and fell. "He must be so lonely and frightened."

They ran into the Court of the Myrtles, slowing down for quick glances along the sides of walls, hoping to find rotational symmetries. Women and children sat around the fishpond in the Court, and the usual chatter dropped to the occasional whisper as they walked in.

Rabab separated herself from her friends and walked over to the girls. She held out her hand, then let it drop. "I am sorry for whatever part I might have had in this matter. I..." She looked away. "I wouldn't willingly cause either of you pain. I didn't realize the waz—" her voice quavered "—that anyone would care about a small dog."

Four tears began to slip one by one down her face. "We, of the harem, must stick together. Our freedom is limited, and our liberties precious. In all my years, and they are many, I have never before betrayed the secrets of the harem. We settle our problems here, not with the outside. I hope you will pardon me. Zoriah knew how upset I was about my birds. I pressed her into telling the sultan and the wazir about all the animals you seemed to be collecting. I don't know why I thought it was so important. I also was young...once."

She took a deep breath. "I would speak to you of Zoriah and let you know that she has petitioned the sultan on your behalf, requesting that the dog be released from the tower and given into your hands. The sultan indicated that the dog is safer where he is. He feels the necessity to seek wisdom from others and from Allah, the Gracious, in this."

The room grew quiet but for the occasional splash of a child's hand in the pond. Ara glanced at Layla before replying formally to her Great Aunt. "I am honored by your concern and love. No one doubts your kindheartedness, not me and not Layla. With so much love around us, all will be well, *inshallah*."

She cradled her head on her aunt's shoulder and whispered, "I'm not angry with you, truly, I'm not."

Rabab sniffed and blinked her eyes in relief. "It's not such a bad dog. I'm sure if we clean him up, you could keep him." She stepped an arm's length away. "Now I should let you get on with your day. I do feel better for having spoken."

Layla reached out and gave Rabab a hug. "You are our cherished elder, the keeper of our traditions, and we love you."

Layla and Ara left the group to climb the stairs, hopeful for a glimpse of the dog. Going from room to room, they found one window that lent a clear view of the Tower. Leaning out the window and tilting their heads up, they saw the tiny form of a dog sitting far above on the wide stone tower windowsill. His head was turned to the sky while he howled mournfully.

"Can you hear me?" Ara called. "Over here."

The howling stopped, and Suleiman's nose turned toward them. His tail wagged back and forth.

Ara leaned out farther and waved her hand back and forth. "He can see us, but we can't talk to him from this distance. At least he knows we care."

Layla grabbed Ara as she tipped halfway out the window. "We should go now. Time is moving fast."

Ara regained her balance and tore herself from the window. "Well, where first? How about we look in the Hall of the Boat?"

Evening came, and though they found a rotational symmetry, it wasn't one that had been broken. Layla had found it in the wooden ceiling of the Hall of the Boat immediately upon entering. Suppertime came and went, and still the girls looked. Suleiman had to change!

The hour was late.

Zoriah entered the hall, her expression of worry not completely masked. It was obvious that she had been tracking them down, bothered that they missed the evening meal yet unable to meet their eyes. In a low, unsteady voice, she said, "Ara, I'm sorry about today. I made a mistake. An error of judgment. We need peace in the harem. You may keep the hound."

"It's too late for that," Ara blurted out. "I need a rotational symmetry example, one that is damaged. It's for our lessons."

There was flicker of confusion before Zoriah steeled her face in repose. "Have you looked in the Gilded Room? There is a symmetry there. Last week, it seemed odd somehow. On the north wall, as I recollect."

Ara tensed in excitement. "We haven't looked there." She looked hopefully at Zoriah.

"Then we should go look now," she said, and set a quick pace while the girls raced alongside her.

The Gilded Room was the loveliest in the Alhambra. Neither Ara nor Layla had been there since the visit from the People of the Book. Memories of the knight with donkey feet still terrified Layla.

As they rounded the corner, Zoriah slowed down and looked up and down the nearest wall. "Now, where is it? Ah, yes." She stopped to look more closely. "See, this is wrong. I don't recall them retiling here, but it is different than I remember." She placed her hand on a row of tile then, frowning, walked across the room to examine the tiles there. "These are not changed. What could have happened?"

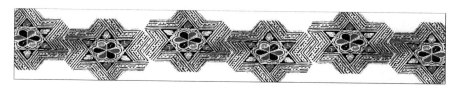

While her back was to it and Ara and Layla watched, the broken symmetry repaired itself. Ara's body shivered as a pulse of energy rippled through the floor. Nearby, lions chuffed to one another.

The girls shot each other a quick look of relief. Suleiman was now transformed. Into what, they did not know—tomorrow they would still have to face the wazir and the sultan. But for now the magic of the rotational symmetry was completed and Suleiman would not live out his days as a hound.

Layla grabbed Zoriah's hand and almost dragged her out of the room. Both girls feared she would see the corrected tile and ask difficult questions.

But as they stood in the corridor, Ara shuffled uncomfortably. Her father's first wife had helped them find the broken rotation symmetry. A debt was owed. "Zoriah, thank you. I shouldn't...I shouldn't have been so cross. Please accept my apology."

"There's been too much misunderstanding and apology in the harem lately," the woman said with the beginning of a smile. "You two need to eat. Let's go and get you supper. We're all under some strain."

Ara squirmed, now wishing she could confide in her father's wife. "Zoriah, please do not mention this to anyone. It's

160

private, and we don't want anyone to know that we search for symmetries. They might laugh."

She gave the girls a quizzical look, but agreed. "There are things in the harem that need to stay here and nowhere else. Today was an example of that."

Outside, high above in the tower, a lone figure blinked into the night at the almost full moon, and restlessly moved across the wide window ledge.

Chapter 34

Though the sun was not yet up, Ara struggled to open her eyes. Su'ah left off stirring the coals and sat down next to her. "So what happened? I knew that dog was trouble. How did you come upon it anyway? I heard the wazir was furious."

She tenderly smoothed Ara's hair. "Child, what were you thinking about getting in the way of so powerful a man?"

Ara sat up on an elbow rubbing her eyes and yawned. "It's not his dog. He's a mean, horrible person." And just like that, she was awake. "What time is it? Is Suleiman all right? Did anything happen while I slept?" She wriggled past Su'ah and grabbed the nearest clothes. "Layla, get up! We have to get to the tower." Her cousin rolled out of bed and wordlessly threw on her clothes.

Su'ah watched in bewilderment. "Suleiman? Is he back? I hadn't heard that he returned."

Ara stopped and collected herself. "No. I just got confused about the dog, that's all."

The older woman was taken aback. "How can you confuse Suleiman with a dirty little hound, even if he is a Turk." She shook her head. "Why must you rise this early anyway?"

"We...we want to make sure the dog is not harmed, that's all."

Su'ah went back to her work. "All this fuss over a dog?"

Dressed, Ara grabbed Layla's hand and half-dragged her out of the room, across the hall and down the way. They leaned far out the window and peered intensely into the pre-dawn. The moon, almost full, still hung in the sky, but the sun had begun to peek over the mountain. A ray of light found the tower and the girls saw something seated on the windowsill. A raptor, its head tucked under its wing. As they watched, it awoke, stretching tall and fanning its tail. Turning restlessly toward the mountains, the golden eagle slowly unfolded his wings one at a time. With his huge, curved beak he preened his feathers carefully then sharply twisted his head toward the Court of the Myrtles. Two piercing eyes locked with the four awestruck ones of the girls, and he nodded in acknowledgment.

The sliver of sun became a crescent. Suleiman stared into the wide, open vista, and with exquisite grace, unfurled his wings, and with a great whoosh, hurled himself off the tower and soared up into the sky. Clinging to the shadows far below, another figure watched, fingering a small broken mirror.

"He's flying toward the mountains." Ara said as Layla watched in silent disbelief. The morning sky lightened with each passing minute. The eagle was disappearing, a small dot far away.

"What's Father going to say when the hound he locked away for safe keeping is missing?"

Layla, still awestruck, looked at her with wide eyes. "What's the wazir going to say, and how do we get Suleiman back?"

"We need Tahirah." Ara grabbed her cousin's hand and together they hurried off in search of the seer.

The call to prayer rang out. They turned to face Mecca and dropped to their knees.

Minutes later, they rose, comfort gained from their morning prayer. Ara was the first to speak. "Let's hurry. We can't find the symmetry until we know what we seek." She looked broodingly toward the mountains. "Suleiman surely will return. He knows how important this is. Then we should go speak with my father."

Tahirah tested her protections again. Someone, she thought with grim remembrance of yesterday's scene, had been trying to break her protections. She felt the discordance that reverberated along her wards. It seemed that the wazir was reaching the end of his tether. How much longer before he snapped entirely? Deep in thought, she moved from ward line to ward line, reinforcing each one, checking their strength.

163

Her servants announced that the girls waited at the door, and Tahirah requested some food for their comfort. At her window, she looked across the Alhambra's vast gardens; the scents of roses and oranges wafting in lifted her spirits. She took a deep breath and, invoking the name of Allah, went to greet Ara and Layla. Within the privacy of her room, the girls exploded in verbal fragments of worry and excitement, finishing with Ara's, "He turned into a golden eagle. The largest I have ever seen."

Layla leaned out the window to look at the distant mountains. "He flew off at dawn, Tahirah. What is the sultan going to do when he finds out the hound is not locked in the tower?"

Tahirah frowned. "I'm more worried about the wazir. He knows Suleiman had to change, but I'm sure he expected him to be trapped in the tower. The wazir is a bitter enemy." She thought back again to yesterday's confrontation. "We have been underestimating the Abd al-Rahmid. Someone has tried to dissolve my wardings. Who else but the wazir?"

She looked each girl in the eye. Her face was absolutely serious, compelling their attention. "You two must stay on your guard. Today is the last day for breaking the spell. Today, you must find two separate symmetry patterns. Just a few hours left to find and repair the first, and then under eight hours left to find the last broken symmetry. Tonight is the end. Finding them is Suleiman's only hope for regaining his human form." She hesitated, debating internally, then spoke very gently, "If you fail and the wazir succeeds, the Alhambra will fall. And us with it, I fear." She closed her eyes, echoes of other times crossing her face.

Her eyes opened. "You two girls must succeed. If the magic is not repaired, we will be faced with a bitter war. Nowhere will it be safe, not even the harem."

Tears trickled slowly down Layla's face. Ara sat staring at her hands, fear for her family entering her mind for the first time. She looked up to ask in a voice edged with worry. "How can we go on with the lessons without Suleiman here?"

Tahirah glanced away, then moved to sit near the tiles. "We must start, even though he must be part of the lesson for the magic to work. His promise is tied to the magic. We will begin and pray he recalls the need to be here. Each shape he turns into has its own animal drives, taking him away from his human self." She whispered low, "He must come to himself soon, *inshallah*, or all is lost."

Tahirah forced herself to concentrate on the task and placed her hand on the tiles. "With this next type of symmetry, glide reflection, you will learn the last motion. So far we have studied three: reflection, translation and rotation. This newest motion is called glide. In it, the symmetry is offset—"

Layla glanced out the window once again and gasped. "I think I see him." Ara joined her and together they scanned the sky. Gliding on a downdraft from the mountains, an eagle circled, coming to land on the tower battlement.

Ara jumped up and down. "Is it him? Is it Suleiman?"

The sharp-eyed eagle peered at them from high above on the battlement, and after surveying the area, flung himself into the air. He spiraled down to their window, landing hard as he struggled for purchase on the flat stone sill. "Ouff."

The bird regained his balance and preened his feathers carefully before eyeing the awestruck group. Ara was the first to gain her tongue. "Suleiman, you're...well...you're beautiful. We're so happy you're safe."

The majestic bird seemed to fill the window. He stood as high as he had as a dog, but the spread of his wings was much wider than either girl was tall.

Tahirah relaxed, relief written across her face. "Welcome, lord of the heavens, you who fly above the clouds and rule the sky. Suleiman, we rejoice that you are here."

The eagle pinned her with his glance. "Gracious Sitti. I should beg your pardon. The lure of the winds carried me far until I recalled my true nature and my promise."

165

Tahirah cocked her head at his tone. "What made you remember?"

He ruffled the feathers on his shoulders. "The lions. I recalled there was a lesson to learn. This one is freedom and responsibility. I came back."

He spread his wings and hopped down onto the floor. He landed in a basin of water, splattering droplets. "We have a task. Let us see to it. We should be teaching glide reflection, is that not so?" One more hop and he marched across the floor. His talons scraped with each step. "Here, follow me," he rasped. "Look at the pattern my feet make as I walk. Yours will make the same pattern, a glide reflection."

Ara slipped off her shoes and walked through the same basin of water before following Suleiman, peering over her shoulder at the footprints she left. "It looks like a horizontal reflection, but the footprints aren't across from one another."

"Exactly." Tahirah said. "It is very similar. The difference is the glide. This pattern moves by first flipping over a horizontal line and then makes a second motion in which it slides—or glides—one position forward."

Ara looked more closely. "Oh, I see. Two motions, first flip and then slide, have to happen, not just one."

The eagle nodded.

Layla, jubilant that Suleiman had returned in time, dipped her feet in the water and proceeded to dance around the room. "I like this symmetry," she said happily, her feet making running patterns across the floor.

Ara moved behind Tahirah, who was still seated near the tiles. "Can we make this symmetry with the tiles now, as we always do?"

Tahirah moved aside and encouraged Ara to take her place. "Here, take these and create a glide reflection." She pointed to six tiles laid upon the floor.

Layla joined Ara, who then whispered in her ear. They went to work.

Ara placed three tiles across the row, spaced apart by the size of a single tile while Layla turned the others, placing each one down across and offset.

The eagle strode over to look. "Good. Now explain how you did it."

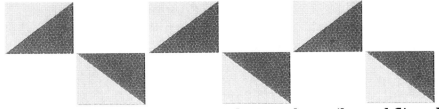

Layla gave him her shy smile. "I took my tiles and flipped them over to get the mirror image of Ara's. Then I moved them, *glided* them, until they lay in the in-between spaces."

"Excellent. That's what I was hoping for," Tahirah said, then glanced uneasily at the sun's position in the sky. "One more symmetry lesson completed. It is still early morning, but you have so little time. We must hurry. It is important for us to speak with your father before he comes looking for us. The wazir can be up to no good."

She turned to the eagle now staring out the window. "Suleiman, what are you planning on doing? In your current form, the girls can't take you with them."

He spread his wings slightly. "I need to eat. I returned to keep my promise, but my body aches with hunger. The small furry ones are often careless in the morning, and I am fast and sharp-eyed."

"Stay out of the wazir's notice. For your life, Suleiman," Tahirah warned. "He is desperate, and his magic surrounds you in whatever form you take. We must not take any unnecessary chances."

He hopped up on the windowsill. His gaze burrowed into her. "Take care yourself. You are here, grounded, while I fly free. Use caution, Sufi. Good hunting." He spread his huge wings and was gone.

Tahirah looked startled by his counsel. "I'll send a servant to find the sultan. We must deal with this the best we can. It will be noticed that the hound is gone."

She bit her lip in concern. "You two need to keep close to the harem. I'll walk you back on my way to speak with your father. While this may not be a pleasant conversation with your father, Abd al-Rahmid may be unable to contain his fury when he sees his quarry has flown. He will be looking not only for Suleiman but also for you."

Chapter 35

As the three entered the Hall of the Kings, Maryam came rushing to greet them, her hijab flowing. "Layla, Ara, I am so sorry about yesterday. Nothing we did would dissuade the wazir. Your father was very exasperated with him."

Ara looked around at the empty hall. "Where is my father?"

"He is closeted with his advisors and can't be interrupted. Some Christians have been speaking with him for the last hour." She clasped and unclasped her hands. "There is a crisis in the mountains not far from here. The town of Lindejarras was torched by renegades. People died, and a caravan traveling through was ransacked."

Tahirah jerked in surprise. "How could that be? I would have heard."

"It must be so." Maryam said. "The foreign men rode hard much of the night to bring him this news. The roads are not safe. Who knows when the next attack might take place."

Tahirah closed her eyes. "I have friends there. I pray to Allah they were not harmed."

"The wazir claims this was inevitable, what with the small number of troops guarding the mountain passes. It is odd, is it not?"

Layla's mother glanced at Ara. "Your father said he must be off immediately. The decision about the dog will have to wait until he returns."

Tahirah frowned. "The sultan is leaving today for the mountains?"

Maryam nodded. "He's preparing to leave now. He wishes to inspect the damage for himself. Even though the mercenaries are gone, he needs to meet with the local officials to aid them in refortifying the town and securing the pass. The caravan carried much needed supplies, wool and grain from Morocco. He wants to see if anything can be salvaged."

Tahirah looked away before casually asking, "Is the wazir going with him?"

Layla's mother shifted uncomfortably. "No, and I'm glad. He apologized to the *shaykh*, right before the messengers arrived. Still, yesterday's incident was unfortunate." She nervously scanned the room before saying quietly, "I don't adhere to spreading fear and rumor, but as you know"—she looked directly in Tahirah's eyes— "Suleiman is missing. And strange and discomforting things seem to happen when the wazir is near. I worry for your safety," she said in a rush. "He is an ambitious man, and there are things in his past..."

Tahirah moved forward to take Maryam's hand. "You are right to be concerned, but take comfort that I have resources of my own. Be assured that I will be safe."

A small shudder ran though Maryam. "I shouldn't have spoken. The wazir overreacted, that's all. He's been agitated lately. He apologized, so it is over. Nonetheless, I'm glad he's off hunting today."

"Hunting?" Tahirah asked in her mildest voice.

"Yes, raptors. It seems an eagle has been carrying off young livestock."

Layla drew in a sharp breath as her mother continued. "He took his bow and arrows and went off with a few soldiers. The two foreigners joined him. Odd, after traveling for so long." She looked thoughtful. "Perhaps it will do some good for the wazir to be away."

"Hunting an eagle?" Ara asked.

Maryam nodded. "I must get back now. Is there anything I can do for you? Would you like to see the dog now? I could try to arrange for you to visit."

Layla eyes widened in panic, while Ara improvised, "I think we shouldn't disturb him. We'll wait until Father gets back."

"Well, if there's nothing more I can do, I'll take my leave of you."

Once Layla's mother disappeared into the palace, Ara turned to Tahirah. "He's trying to kill Suleiman, isn't he?"

The mathemagician looked off toward the mountains before nodding. "I'm afraid so. Somehow the wazir knows Suleiman has become an eagle. There is no eagle killing livestock. It's an excuse. The Alhambra's magic is tied to Suleiman, and time is running out for the wazir."

Ara stared off to the mountains, panic written across her face. Layla looked down, trying to hide her tears.

"One problem resolved, and another created." Tahirah shook her head. "But we must not give in to despair. Even should he find Suleiman, eagles soar very high, higher than most can shoot." She gave the girls an encouraging pat. "Quickly, now, you must search for the glide reflections. I will attempt to locate Suleiman by my magic and call him back. I don't know how successful I will be in contacting an eagle, but I must try." She shook her head again. "Evil mathemagics wastes so much time and energy. So great a misuse of Allah's wisdom." She turned to leave, enveloped in her cloak. "Come to my rooms if you need me before you find the broken glide reflection. May Suleiman return soon, *inshallah*. Remember," she looked at them sharply. "Stay away from the wazir!"

Ara tried to concentrate on where best to start. But visions of an eagle, wounded, lying crumpled on the ground, kept flitting across her mind. Layla stood, looking back in the direction of her mother's leave-taking.

"I should tell her," she murmured to her cousin. "But she would worry so."

Ara looked toward the palace. "Tomorrow. Tomorrow we tell her and my father everything. He will be back, Suleiman will be human again, and the wazir..." She hesitated. "Father *must* return by tomorrow," she hissed, rubbing her forehead. "Let's get started." She turned one last time to search the sky for Suleiman before going inside.

Their time in the Hall of the Kings yielded nothing. Ara noticed tiny cracks in the ceilings that were hidden within the drawings that adorned the room. She shivered, afraid.

They rushed through the Court of the Lions and passed the great carved doors of the Hall of the Abencerrajes. Sunlight poured into the room through the star-cut ceiling. They walked slowly around the low fountain and looked carefully at every row of tiles, hoping a glide reflection design would leap out. Ara chose the north wall, while Layla focused on the south end of the room.

Ara found herself unable to focus. *The wazir is going to kill Suleiman,* she thought, biting her lip. *Suleiman is busy searching for food and he doesn't know the wazir is hunting him. What if Suleiman becomes lost and doesn't return?*

She and Layla walked across the Court of the Lions toward the Hall of the Two Sisters, nodding to the lions as they passed.

I need to find Suleiman. Ara thought about the high outer walls of the palace. *I bet I could climb over the palace walls and find him. He'd come as soon as he saw her, she felt sure. Then the wazir would never find him.* She started smiling to herself as a plan began to take shape. *I will be like the Prophet's favorite wife A'isha, who led the Battle of the Camel. A true Muslim heroine.*

There was a wonderfully branched tree near the far north wall. It wasn't securely guarded in the middle of the day. She could scamper up and get to the top of the outside wall. The stables must have a rope. She could be over, find Suleiman and get back before anyone notices. She hummed quietly, a new lilt to her walk.

Behind her, a shape disconnected itself from the fountain and stealthily trailed after her.

In the Hall of the Two Sisters, Layla found a glide reflection and showed it to her cousin. Ara nodded, distracted. *How was she ever going to get across the wall walkway?*

Layla cocked her head. "Are you all right? You have been muttering to yourself for the last quarter hour. You're not planning anything dangerous, are you?" Suspicion had crept into her voice.

Ara frowned. "Don't be silly. Of course I'm thinking, but nothing dangerous. We need to go by the stables. There are tiles on the floor we should check."

Layla missed a step. "The stables, but...Tahirah told us to stay near the harem."

"You can stay. But I'm going." Ara moved quickly out the doors and headed toward the stables. After a moment's hesitation, Layla followed.

Ara knew what she had to do. The wazir was out hunting Suleiman, and she needed to protect her friend. She frowned and picked up the pace. Layla trailed behind, asking, "Are you sure we need to go there?"

Ara nodded, focused on the stable and her plans. As they rounded the corner of the garden, the stables came into view and she smiled in anticipation.

Layla placed her hand on her friend's shoulder. "Promise, promise me you're not thinking of doing anything risky."

Ara shrugged her hand off. "Stop. I'll be right out. You stay here in case someone comes." She crept quietly into the back of the stables. The horses snuffled at her, looking for treats and a rub on the nose.

She grabbed a rope and a long piece of cotton cloth and slung both over her shoulder, then grabbed a small bow and quiver from the wall.

When Ara emerged, Layla looked aghast. "What have—no! It's too dangerous."

Ara trotted to the base of the high palace walls and checked the lower branches of the tree as she tied the cloth into a passable turban. "This isn't the first time I've climbed this."

"You can't leave the Alhambra. Think of what your father would say. Please, we have to finish finding the symmetries. You promised Tahirah!"

Rearranging the rope and bow onto her back, Ara countered, "I'm going to find Suleiman. I'm not going to let the wazir hurt him, and that's that." She set her jaw and turned her back.

"You can't go." Layla grabbed her cousin's arm. "What about the magic? You need to find it *here*."

Ara shook her off before reaching upward to the tree. She placed her foot on a low, thick branch. "If Suleiman's dead, the magic doesn't matter anymore. The Alhambra will fall. Remember what Tahirah said? Only his changing back to his human form can save it. I'm going. Don't try to stop me. If Suleiman dies and the Alhambra's magic fails, it'll be my fault."

Layla gasped, and Ara felt someone tugging on the other end of the rope. "Layla, stop it. I must go."

"That isn't me," her cousin said in a hushed voice. "I think you better let go of that tree."

Chapter 36

Ara felt hot breath on her neck and nervously turned to see a mouth with many large teeth curved in an angry snarl. A lion stood with one foot on her rope and stared at her, unblinking.

"Child of the Alhambra," he rumbled, "your duty is here. Do you abandon your obligations so readily?"

Ara blinked. Her lion! Her fingers slipped from the branch, and she fell to the ground with a thud. Layla stared openmouthed at the lion, relieved in a frightened sort of way. Gold sparkled in his mane. His feet and legs seemed covered in quartz; the long curved claws, ivory. His eyes shone with the fire of coal turning into diamonds; his fur glistened like mica. Ara gazed at him in wonder. Finally, she grinned and shook herself, blissfully disregarding his reproach. "You're here and talking to me! I have been hoping for so long that you would."

He was silent for some time before he spoke again. "Do you so weary of your responsibilities that you let others down and quit?"

She stiffened at the criticism. "No, not at all. I'm not quitting, I'm going to rescue Suleiman!"

"By leaving the palace, you put yourself at risk. Without you, there will be no healing of the Alhambra, and Suleiman will never return to his normal shape. You put all in peril to soothe your own desires and fears." He glared at her in disapproval. "There are times to hunt and times to remain silent while danger walks the paths."

She frowned back. That wasn't so. She wasn't soothing her own fears. Suleiman could be in danger. She wasn't making it up.

The voice rumbled again. "You have not found the broken symmetry. Do you believe the earth will stop turning because you wish it?"

Ara replied. "No, but..."

"But...?" he snarled. "Tell me how you were going to get back to the Alhambra before the sands of time ran out. You with two feet and no wings."

"I'm quick. I would be back soon," she insisted, more and more annoyed at her lion's disapproval. Maybe she shouldn't have wished to speak to him. She liked him better when he was silent.

He sat down and started casually licking his paw, one foot still on her rope. "Is it that you have no trust in Suleiman? Do you think him reckless?"

"No, Suleiman is very capable," Ara had to admit. "He is careful and thoughtful."

"Unlike some whom we love whose nature runs to impulse." The lion winked at Layla, who watched the debate, scarcely breathing. He shifted his weight, releasing the rope. "Yet quickness of mind and spirit are admirable qualities in a cub. Such cubs grow into lions with intelligence and leadership. There are times in the hunt when it is good to sprint, to react fast and change directions. There are other times to quietly lay with your pack and study your prey. This is one of those times. You need to remain steadfast and trust that Suleiman also keeps to his task." The lion snarled suddenly, uneasy. "I must go. The wazir's magic presses in on me. Find the symmetries." Silver lights twinkled as he began to disappear. "Suleiman and the wazir both return from the north."

"Wait! Does the wazir have Suleiman? What's happening? Wait, your name, what's your name?"

A whispered growl drifted across the air. "The wazir's magic constricts my brothers and me. Break the bonds and complete the magic so we may also do our duty."

Ara sat stunned on the ground. "But I still don't know your name."

Layla, her eyes still huge, reached down to tug her cousin up. "Ara, your lion! He is so beautiful and huge! Those teeth..." She took a breath. "What should we do now?"

Ara stood, not quite able to meet her cousin's eyes. "We find the symmetry. But we shouldn't heal it until we know where Suleiman is and that he is safe." She was quiet for a moment. "Cousin, I am sorry I did not listen to you. You were right."

Layla looked at her with pain-filled eyes and whispered. "I didn't know what to do. I kept thinking about the dangers outside and that you might get hurt."

Ara flinched and reddened. Layla gave her a hug. "We are friends as well as cousins. All is well between us."

Ara grinned in relief before grabbing the equipment from the ground. "Let us go, then." She looked at the bow and rope in her hand, then looked around in dismay. "I'll return these as soon as Suleiman is back and transformed." Hastily she and Layla stuffed the tools deep into a hedge of low bushes and, after a last look, hurried toward the palace.

On the way, Ara mulled over her exchange with her lion. Maybe it was true that she needed to be more careful and less hasty. Still, it was nice he implied she might grow up to be a leader. She *would* stay with this task. She *did* trust that Suleiman would outsmart the wazir.

They entered the Palace of the Myrtles and crossed the stone floor to stop at the fishpond. "I'll start here and work my way around the courtyard." Ara said. "Where do you want to look?"

"Maybe the Hall of the Boat, as it is close."

Ara nodded agreement.

The girls separated. Layla called out that she found a symmetry, but a moment later she amended, "No, I was mistaken. The pattern isn't quite right. There's a glide, but no reflection. And it isn't broken."

Ara walked slowly around the courtyard pond, still thinking about the lion's counsel. *It wasn't that he said she shouldn't be spontaneous, just that she should be more careful. That didn't seem so bad.* She saw a series of tiles and grinned as she mentally followed the motion across the row. Glide, reflect, glide, reflect—over and over.

Layla tugged on her sleeve. "Let's go to the tower and look for Suleiman. You mustn't repair the broken symmetry. Not until he is here and safe."

Chapter 37

From the tower, the girls watched as an eagle winged toward the palace, skimming through the clouds. Ara heard distant trumpets. She peered down the road and saw men-at-arms riding fast. At the head, riding a big-boned chestnut mare, was the wazir. His body twisted as he searched the skies.

Please let him not see Suleiman, Ara fervently prayed. Just then the eagle dipped down through a cloud and a cry went up from one of the hunters, who pointed upwards. The bowmen loosed three arrows in rapid succession. The eagle soared above them, their barbs sailing harmlessly below.

The wazir waved his arms, cursing his men. As two archers raced on ahead, he yanked his reins back hard and flung himself to the ground, pulling out an object from his saddlebags. Light reflected off it, and Ara gasped in recognition. He raised the mirror to the sky and began chanting.

"Layla, he's doing black mathemagics! That's what he did before. He used a mirror just like he is now.

"Suleiman," Ara shouted, thrusting herself half out of the window, "look out!"

The eagle veered, and the magic whooshed by in the form of a small black cloud. It hung there; two songbirds flew through it and disappeared. Dark shadows twisted inside the cloud and feathers exploded into the air. The eagle's eyes locked onto the wazir, bent over his mirror below.

Layla and Ara gasped as Suleiman suddenly pinned in his wings and hurtled down from the sky.

Too late, the wazir looked up and discovered that he who had been the predator was now the prey. He shrieked and flung his hands over his face.

Layla screamed.

Just before he crashed into the wazir, Suleiman pulled out of his dive and, extending his talons, grabbed the mirror. His

179

talons raked the wazir's hand. Blood spurted. Abd al-Rahmid shrieked as claws ripped through his flesh. His companions turned at the noise, dumbfounded.

Doubled over in pain, he shrieked at his men to kill the eagle. One man hurried to his aid, while the other notched his bow. Clutching the mirror, Suleiman flapped harder, his strong wings pumping as he tried to distance himself from the deadly arrows arching in his direction.

Layla hid her eyes behind her hands. Ara watched Suleiman fly over the palace walls, dodging arrows until he was inside the palace boundaries. She leaned over to reassure her cousin. Just then, one last arrow shot upward and nicked his tail feathers, sending him into an airborne somersault. The mirror flew out of his claws, and he spiraled down from the sky, all grace gone. By sheer strength, he managed to slow his fall to a sluggish, if wobbly, descent. From her vantage point, Ara could hear the wazir screaming at the men.

Ara turned to her cousin and saw, lit by the sun, a broken symmetry on the far wall. As the tile turned to match the others, the lions began to roar. The Alhambra itself rumbled, the palace healing—and suddenly Ara knew what would happen. She ran to the window.

With a startled squawk, Suleiman lost what little control he had, plummeting toward the ground as he changed into a new form in mid air. Both Layla and Ara leaned out the window, aghast at the blurred vision of airborne fur and flailing legs. Falling, falling, too quickly.

Fear grabbed at Ara's chest. She couldn't breathe. What if he was badly hurt? What if he died?

Then Suleiman—whatever he had become—disappeared behind the stables.

The girls tore down the stairs and outside. As they rounded the back of the stables, the girls stopped. There was only a pile of hay. Suleiman was nowhere to be seen. As they looked helplessly at each other, a low moan came from within the pile. Ara yelped, and they dug frantically through the hay for their friend.

"Suleiman, can you hear me?" Layla called. "Are you hurt?"

A shaky voice responded, "I'm as well as can be expected after falling from such a height. The wind is knocked out of me, though. You need to be more careful, Ara! Did you not see how high up I was?"

She dug faster. "I'm sorry, Suleiman. It was an accident."

He coughed, sounding like he was spitting out straw from his mouth. "I only wish there was space for some discipline and caution between your curiosity and your impulsiveness."

The girls scooped more hay to the side, digging deeper.

He coughed again, rattling around within the center of the haystack. "Well, let us go forward. Your nature can't be changed in—"

"Hurry," Ara interrupted, tired of the lecture. "The wazir and his men are outside the palace, but they will be upon us searching for you any minute. We need to get you out of here and hidden." She tried to peer through the straw. "I didn't mean to see the symmetry. I didn't even know it was there. Are you sure you're all right?"

The haystack moved. From it emerged a large pile of straw draped over spindly legs. Suleiman lifted his head, and a tangle of straw rose in the air. A small golden haystack encompassing his head and shoulders shifted around him. "I'm a lion, aren't I? I can feel my glorious mane and tail." He tossed his head. "I knew each transformation brought me closer to my own true self, but I never dared hope for so much. Without doubt, I am blessed. No longer must I run and hide from evil. My roar of challenge will be heard for miles. He reared back, hay flying every which way, and drew in a breath. "Bleeeat!" He stopped short. "That's wrong. Must have a bit of straw caught in my throat." He cleared his windpipe. "Ehh, ehhh. There, that's better. Ahem." He took another deep breath. "Bleeeat!"

The haystack slipped sideways, and a small black horn poked up out of the debris.

"Suleiman, I don't think you're a lion."

"Not a lion? But...Ah, well, what am I then, a mighty steed or...?"

The girls looked at one another in growing dismay.

"Suleiman," Layla said gently, "you have horns. I think, well, I think you're a goat."

The straw-covered eunuch-goat stiffened in incredulity. A short tail flicked beneath the hay. "No, that's not right. You're mistaken. Perhaps I'm some exotic animal you are unaware of." He shook his head and straw flew everywhere. Two triangular eyes peered worriedly out at them. "I'm a wildebeest, mayhap. They have horns. Or maybe a dragon from the Far East—I heard of them once..."

Ara shook her head, trying to hide a smile. "A goat."

"No." He stamped his foot. "I've already had a lesson in humility. One was more than sufficient."

Suleiman turned his head, looking in growing horror at his body, which was undeniably that of a middle-sized black goat. A small, stringy beard framed an increasingly disgusted expression upon his face. Tiny black hooves stamped a beat of frustration. "I simply won't have it," he declared and dove back under the straw. "I'm not coming out until I've changed into something suitable."

"Suleiman, I don't think throwing a tantrum is going to help." Ara reached in and grabbed a horn with both hands. "Really, you have to come out. Now! We have to find a safe place for you to hide. The wazir is searching for you."

"No, no, no!"

Layla dug into the hay and, lifting the straw off Suleiman, stared sympathetically into his eyes. "This is your last shape. We have less than eight hours left. Suleiman, truly we need you. By tonight, you will be back to your own most suitable form, but we must hurry."

"But," he insisted, backing farther into the hay, pulling Ara along, "it's just not right."

The clatter of men and horses on cobblestones pushed both the girls into a panic.

Ara hauled desperately at his horn. "Suleiman, you can be a live goat now or you can be a dead goat when the wazir arrives. Please, we must leave *now*!"

Reluctantly, Suleiman clambered out of the hay and shook himself. A quick, disgusted look reconfirmed his goat shape. "How long do I have to be a...?" He couldn't quite bring himself to say it.

"Goat," Ara finished for him. She pulled him along the path toward Tahirah's. Layla put her arm across his back, wrinkling her nose at the strong goat smell.

"Hurry, I hear voices!" Ara urged.

"I'm coming." But Suleiman dragged his feet as he noted the direction they headed. "Must we go to the Palace of the Partal? I don't want anyone to see me in this state, particularly not Tahirah."

Many footsteps crunched the stones on the path beyond.

Ara blanched at the nearing sounds. "No time to run."

Frightened and miserable, Layla agreed.

Ara looked around for a safe place to hide. The stables; many dark corners, and a goat there would not be unusual. They ducked inside.

The horses nickered at the girls but snorted at Suleiman. Layla climbed the narrow stairs to the loft with Ara pushing Suleiman close behind. The room was silent but for the sound of horses chewing and the occasional rustle of a mouse.

"Maybe they are searching the gard—" Ara broke off when the big stable door creaked open. Layla shivered and edged closer to Ara.

"We'll check the stables," a voice called. The straw rustled and a horse whinnied; soldiers passed, swords drawn, poking and peering into each stall. "God's blood, no damaged animal here," the beefy man said in Castilian Spanish. "The Grenadan wazir is becoming stranger and stranger."

The thin man with the bushy eyebrows removed the saddle from his horse and rubbed him briskly with his blanket. "I'll be glad when this is over. All this sneaking around in enemy territory makes me nervous. The sultan looked at us so hard, I was certain he saw through our story."

Layla put a trembling hand on Ara to steady her as they peered down through the slated eaves.

The other man lifted a halter from a hook. "You worry too much. Soon the trap will spring and the sultan will be caught. What do you think the King wants him for, ransom or death?"

Ara started slightly. Reluctantly she met Layla's eyes, now wide with fear.

"I neither know nor care. I just have to get this map and message to the army before midnight. Our men will surround the sultan at dawn. Right when they are all crouched in devotion to their Islamic God." He laughed.

Ara looked back at Suleiman. Her father would die. She trembled, praying to Allah that they would not succeed. She must get to Tahirah with the information and—

Suleiman's ears perked up. "I've got to get that paper," he whispered, and before the girls could grab him, he turned and stumbled down the stairs into the stable hall, chewing on a bit of hay.

"What's that?" The thin soldier swung around, his sword grasped in both his hands.

184

"Just a goat, you fool, looking for food. Relax. Put the map away, we need to leave."

The soldier placed the paper in his saddlebag, closing the flap firmly. "Get out of my way," he yelled at the goat as both men ambled out of the doors. The moment they entered the paddock, Suleiman raced for the saddlebag and deftly opened the pocket with his teeth.

"Hurry," Ara hissed at Layla, still climbing cautiously down the ladder.

While Suleiman frantically nosed the contents of the saddlebag, the girls stood in indecision.

Suleiman flicked his eyes at the girls and bleated, his muffled voice not to be ignored. "Run now, out the side door." Startled, they moved to flee. He grabbed the map and tugged. A corner of the map edged out. Ara, looking over her shoulder beyond Suleiman, whispered urgently, "They're coming back!"

He pulled harder, ripping the paper. Suleiman nosed the flap back down and galloped out the door, only half of the map clenched between his teeth.

185

Chapter 38

Layla's harsh, uneven breathing came from behind Ara. They had run for a long time, racing from shadow to shadow. Ignoring Suleiman's grumbling under his breath about lessons and magic, Ara clutched the ripped map in her hand. A pungent, musty goat smell reminded her that they needed to hide him. Hearing no more footsteps, she peered around a large olive tree. After a careful look, they all rushed from bush to bush until they came up to the inner palace wall. From there, Ara edged up to a corner of the palace and stuck her head around the side. "All clear." She waved them forward, still looking out for the wazir and his hunting companions.

When none of the guards challenged the trio, she felt her hopes rise.

Suleiman backed up into the bushes. "I'll wait here for you. You can give Tahirah the map."

Ara gave him an uncompromising look. "You have to come with us. We need you there for the lesson."

Scooting from building to building, the girls pushed, pulled and prodded the reluctant goat onward. Suleiman argued with them the whole time.

With only a short dash between them and Tahirah's rooms, the sound of raised voices echoed down the path. The girls ducked behind a wooden gate as the wazir, coddling his injured hand, strode forth with four sentries. "You! Guard this building. Don't let anyone in," he said of Tahirah's rooms. "And you, find that animal now."

"What animal?" a sentry asked in a bewildered voice.

"What animal?" The wazir whirled on the poor man. "I don't know what it is now. A *damaged* animal. It was struck with an arrow. Find it!"

The men looked furtively at each other before one responded, "But, Wazir, what about the eagle? That was what we shot."

The wazir's voice got even louder. "Are you challenging me? Find that animal. It may be with the sultan's daughter and niece. Take it from them and kill it!"

Layla gasped and the wazir jerked his head around toward the noise. "What was that?"

Ara clasped her hand over Layla's mouth and pulled her back into the shadows of the garden. Suleiman examined the scraped spot on his tail where the arrow had nicked him.

The guards looked at each other in dismay. "The wind, Abd al-Rahmid, nothing more."

The wazir ground his teeth. "You two, check over there. You, recheck the stables. I was sure he fell over there. He has to be around here somewhere. You stay here and let no one in to see the Sufi witch. She must be involved somehow."

His voice changed then, "Guard the harem entrance. The sultan's daughter may seek to return there. Something is broken in the Court of the Lions, and I need to speak with her."

With that he marched to the front of the Palace of the Partal and banged on the door.

Ara and Layla's eyes met.

The girls crept deeper into the garden, trying to muffle the sound of Suleiman's goat feet. When they were far enough away, Layla whispered in Ara's ear. "Does that mean that the final broken symmetry is there?"

"I don't know. Maybe. But his voice sounded funny. Sly."

Layla twisted her tunic hem in her hands. "He always sounds so to me."

"True."

"Now what? Where do we hide?"

Ara bit her lip. "We need to go to the harem, but first we need to see Tahirah. She's stronger in magic then he is. We'll be safe there. And we still need to learn the final symmetry."

"But how do we get in to her? He stands at the door."

Ara thought that over, then grinned. "The same way Suleiman did in eagle form, except we climb."

A short time later, Layla teetered on her cousin's shoulder, stretching for the window ledge of Tahirah's sleeping rooms. "Hurry up," Ara hissed. "You're heavy."

"I can touch the sill, but I'm not high enough to pull myself in," Layla whispered back, struggling.

Ara's face was bright red from exertion. "Can you see Tahirah?"

Layla grunted, "I'm not tall enough, and I don't hear her."

Suleiman looked at the two girls and puzzled over their difficulty. "Layla, can you bend over a bit?" She ducked her head and hunched her shoulders. Suleiman delicately leapt onto Ara, lightly touched Layla shoulders as he bounded into the window. "That was easy." Ignoring the girls' comments about his unexpected weight, he peered down from the windowsill. "I forgot, goats can scale anything. I'll find Tahirah and return soon."

Layla jumped down, and Ara collapsed in a heap. "Ugh, you are heavier than I thought." They dusted themselves off and clung nervously to the dark corners of the wall.

"Ara, Layla," came a whispered call. "I'm sending a long piece of fabric down. Wait while I tie it to a column." Layla's face was pinched and white, sure that the wazir would stride around the corner any second.

Tahirah leaned out, scanning the area. She held her hand to her lips for them to be silent. Then she threw down a length of cloth that she had knotted and twisted for strength. "Here, climb up, but be quiet. The wazir and his men are on the south side of the building."

Soon both girls were seated on the floor of Tahirah's apartments. Ara checked her hands for scrapes and scratches. Layla sat petting the goat while Tahirah stood by the window searching the landscape, her usual calm demeanor strained.

"The wazir dare not force his way into my quarters, but he made quite a fuss banging at the door. All the servants were asked if they had seen the two of you. Fortunately, none of them had. We must complete our lesson immediately and get you two back safe in the harem."

Ara leapt up, waving the map. "But Tahirah, he's setting a trap for Father. They're going to ambush him. At dawn, they said."

Tahirah took the ripped, crumpled paper and began examining it. "We heard them," Ara went on, "when we were hiding in the stables. They're planning to capture him."

"It's a map of the country south of here, near Lindejarras. Here is the seal of the Castile king." Tahirah's finger traveled down the paper. "There it is, 'capture the Alhambra sultan at...' then it is ripped.

"It was a trap all along." She turned it over. "It does not mention the wazir—at least, the piece we have here doesn't." She sighed and her hands collapsed in her lap. "Too many urgencies in one day. Well, first things first. We must complete the last lesson."

Ara turned white. "But my father, they'll take him as ransom, won't they?"

Tahirah shook her head, "No, not now. With this paper as proof, I will go to the commander of the guard. We'll find the sultan tonight, before this trap is sprung. And without alerting the wazir."

Layla leaned forward. ""But these are the last hours we have to break the spell."

Tahirah closed her eyes and breathed deeply, her lips moving in a quick appeal to Allah. Returning to the present, she whispered in a voice that bordered on prayer, "Except to save the sultan, I would not leave you two alone tonight. But know I will return to you by midnight, if at all possible."

Ara sat down suddenly. "What about Suleiman? Where can he stay?" She frowned at her horned friend. "I don't know what Zoriah and Su'ah would say."

Layla hid her worry beneath a hesitant smile. "Actually, you know exactly what they'd say."

Looking at the goat, Tahirah shook her head. "Let us complete the lesson, and then we will worry about how to hide, um, Suleiman. That is the least of our worries right now. Thank Allah, the beneficent, the tiles are here, just where we left them this morning. The last symmetry example." She carefully sorted the tiles into a select pile of ten. "Here, I think this will do. Glide with a vertical mirror," she said, laying them across the floor. "The pattern is as follows—"

"No, wait, I see it," Ara jumped in. "May I describe it?"

The mathemagician smiled her slow smile. "Of course, child, go ahead."

"Well, it starts with a triangle that already has flipped over a vertical line." Ara looked at Tahirah, who nodded encouragement. "And then, well, it glides to a new position and flips over a horizontal line."

Suleiman butted her gently with his horn. "That's my girl. Glide, flip." He bobbed his head emphatically.

Layla lay on her stomach to more closely observe the pattern. "But, it also rotates. It's like the double reflection in that if you look at it upside down it looks the same." She looked up, her eyes bright with confidence.

Everyone turned to the dainty dark-eyed girl. Suleiman blinked. Tahirah shook her head in amazement. "The girl who thought she couldn't do mathematics. Layla, that is very clever of you. Yes, it could be seen as rotating. In fact that is one of the differences between the glide reflection symmetry and this one. Even though there is a rotation, the way we define the movement of this symmetry is in the glide and flip movements.

"The other difference is that this pattern *always* starts with a symmetrical object, one that reflects. That object then glides and flips again. The glide reflection always starts with an *asymmetric* object."

Bang! bang! The noise echoed all the way from the front of the palace, through the closed doors and into Tahirah's room. Gazes meeting, the girls started to rise.

"You must leave," Tahirah whispered before calling, "Yes, who is it?"

The servant's voice sounded frightened. "It's the wazir again. He demands to see you, *Sitti*. What should we do? He's banging on the front door, and soldiers are with him."

Ara and Layla blanched and the goat backed up toward the window. Tahirah's lips were white, but she kept her voice even to her servant while anxiously pushing the children and Suleiman to the window. "Send a runner to search out the sultan's other advisors, and then please invite the wazir in. Inform him that I will be out as soon as I am presentable."

Ara grabbed Tahirah's hand. "We heard the wazir talking. We think the last broken symmetry may be in the Court of the Lions."

Bam! Bam! The noise came again.

Tahirah pulled away. "Right now, you need to be safe. Get to the harem as soon as possible. It's the only place he can't go."

"But what about the Court of the Lions? The last symmetry?"

Tahirah's body was turned toward her door as if expecting it to open. "Look in the harem; possibly the symmetry is there. If not..." She left it unsaid. The Alhambra would fall.

"I'll contact you as soon as I return."

"Hurry," Tahirah pressed. "Climb down as quickly and quietly as you can. The wazir has men checking each door. I'll distract him as long as I can. Here." She handed Ara a shapeless gray hijab. "Take this. It belongs to one of my handmaidens. Perhaps one of you can disguise yourself in it.

"Suleiman, you're going to have to jump. As soon as you're safely away, I'll go to the door to meet the wazir."

Ara climbed down first, with Layla right behind. Suleiman, after a slight pause, closed his eyes and launched himself from the window ledge, landing with an "ouff" on the ground. Ara bent over Suleiman, reassuring herself that he was not hurt before the trio sprinted for the gardens.

All three of them were out of breath; they stopped for a rest beside a small stream deep in the Alhambra. In the low light of dusk, the gracefully spreading trees looked ominous—fingers and limbs reaching out. The one-eyed stare of the moon, rising up from the horizon, glared at them as if in reproach. Even the magical sound of the nightingales felt more akin to a dirge than a ballad.

Suleiman, bruised from his adventures, bent stiffly to lap water from the stream before collapsing next to Ara. She listened to him mutter over and over to himself, "But what lesson could I learn as a goat?"

She wrapped her arms about her chest to ward off the chill. A pattern on the low wall near the stream had caught her eye as she stumbled over a hedge. A glide with a vertical mirror, but not a broken one.

192

Layla, shivering with fear and cold, tugged Tahirah's hijab up around her shoulders. "We've got to get in the harem."

Ara rubbed her nose in frustration and exhaustion. "Yes, but how? We can't just dance in with a goat! If we reach the entrance, we could get in but for Suleiman..." She looked at her cousin contemplatively, and then back at Suleiman. Amusement danced across her face.

Layla looked at her in growing alarm. "Whatever you're thinking, I'm against it."

"Suleiman, can you stand on your hind legs?"

He barely looked up from his exhausted sprawl. "Yes, most goats can. That's how they strip leaves off trees for food."

"Could you walk on your hind legs by yourself?"

Something about her voice caught his attention. "Why do you ask?" He tracked her glance to the crumpled hijab. Then he rose to all four feet, quivering. "I won't! That's, well—that's wrong!"

"You have to! We will hold you up, won't we, Layla?"

Layla stared at her cousin in both admiration and horror. "Ara, if we are caught—"

"If we get caught by the wazir, we are truly dead." She said. "We might be able to get into the harem this way. There's no way we can walk in with a goat!"

Chapter 39

Tahirah drew herself together. Her power was contained and focused. Control was the key here, control and mastery of herself. She needed to buy time for the girls to escape, and yet it was imperative that she warn the sultan before he was ambushed. She wrapped herself in her white cloak, opened the door and walked down the staircase to the room below. The wazir was there, glaring at her servants. Six of the Alhambra guards were behind him. "Seize her," he said. "She is a witch and a traitor. She hides unnatural things in her room. Even the sultan's daughter is under her spells."

Tahirah sighed as she might with a particularly difficult child. "This is unnecessary, al-Rahmid. You overstep yourself. I am under the sultan's protection. No one, not even you, can defy that." She smiled at the guards, who hesitated to approach a woman and one so well respected at that. "Please, go forth and search. There is nothing to find. And if two of you would stay near—" She searched for the right words. "al-Rahmid is not himself."

He turned red. "Witch, you will await the sultan's return in the dungeons."

She raised her palm toward the approaching guards and quietly sat down. Her voice lowered, magic rolling out to resonate with their sense of honor. "There is no need for you to accost me, a woman not of your family." She looked at each of them in turn. "As I am accused of something that cannot be proved, I would not put you in jeopardy of our laws. I will not try to escape or run. Here I am, and I will remain here until the Commander of the Army comes. He has been summoned and will be here forthwith. If you wish to wait with me, I will have tea ordered." She gave them an expectant look before sending a servant scurrying off for tea. The guards shifted nervously and glanced back at the wazir.

Eyes fixed on her, he spoke to the guard, his voice menacing, "Leave us. Two of you stand guard at the door. Let no one enter or leave." The guards cast a quick look at Tahirah, who looked serenely back, and then they bowed out of the room.

"al-Rahmid," Tahirah said once they were alone. "Do not continue down this path."

"Enough, woman!" He took three quick strides across the room. But through the walls, a ghostly lion slithered, and then another, until all twelve lions had entered. A low steady growl came from them as they circled the room. Tahirah breathed a sigh of relief. Though the wazir's magic still held, it was slipping. The lions no longer slept, and their presence gave her confidence. She tapped the ground lightly with her foot. Her magic spilled across the room, and the floor before her cracked and glowed red-hot. The wazir came to a halt a pace away staring at the fire and the lions.

"This is not well done, al-Rahmid. You forget who I am. I know what you plan. It cannot be." She pierced him with her gaze. "The time has not yet come for the fall of Granada, and you are not to be the agent of it. All you are doing is causing pain and suffering, betraying those who trusted you. Turn from this now. There is still hope for you."

As he stood, flickers of flame inched toward him, slowly circling round. The lions roared louder. Fear and pride crossed his face. "This will not contain me for long. What are you scheming?"

The door thundered with blows.

"*Sitti*, Tahirah, are you within?" Layla's father, the Commander of the Army, called out.

She looked steadfastly at al-Rahmid. "Choose now, and choose carefully."

His face contorting, he backed away. "I have chosen. This day is mine!" He turned and strode quickly out the easterly door.

Chapter 40

Ara carefully evaluated her work. The creature dressed in a hijab stared back at her. One hoof, hidden in the folds of material, lightly rested on Layla's shoulder. "Walk forward again and, this time keep your tail tucked under. It looks peculiar when it sticks out."

Two eyes glared daggers at her. Layla started forward with Suleiman clomping after. Ara sighed. "Can't you be more graceful? Don't hunch over so much. You don't walk much like a girl."

Layla muttered softly, "He doesn't move like anything human."

Suleiman tucked his tail and tried to stand upright. He snarled under his breath, and took two slow, tottering steps. "This isn't going to work. The guards will see right through this."

Ara grimaced. "It will have to do. At least it's near dark. Let's go. Keep your head down. No one would believe those eyes are human."

They rounded the corner. A guard coming from the other direction cried, "Halt, Sultan's child. The wazir wishes you brought to him."

Ara gulped and forgot to breathe, her wits too frightened to work. Just as she opened her mouth, hoping some useful words would come out, a small, shrouded figure prodded the guards back with her cane.

"Since when do you take orders from Abd al-Rahmid? And since when are women's affairs any of his never-mind?" Rabab, enshrouded in her dark brown hijab, stood her ground while the three cohorts continued their unsteady progress across the walk. Zoriah stood behind, her face hidden but her eyes unwavering. Secure in her rights, her posture defied the guard to harm the old woman.

"I...I...*Sitti*, I must," the guard stammered, shifting from foot to foot.

196

"You must!" Rabab said shaking a finger under his nose. "*You* must mind your own business and stay out of the harem's affairs. Have you added bullying girls to your work?"

The guard flinched before the hunched old woman. "But, the wazir ordered me to bring—"

"And, in the sultan's absence, I am ordering you to go about your business," Rabab retorted as the trio hurried through the doorway. "No one who isn't of the harem is to enter," she pointed out, "and no man has the right to meddle in our affairs." She placed herself in the doorway, blocking his view after Ara, Layla and Suleiman entered. "Now, leave us in peace." Turning her back on him, she walked away; and Zoriah firmly closed the door on the gawking guard.

From the doorway, Ara saw a cluster of children inspecting Suleiman. Hasan looked quizzically at the robed goat, tilting his head to one side. Jada's eyes dropped down to Suleiman's feet. Ara backed across the room and whispered to Layla to disappear and meet her later. Too much attention was being given to Suleiman, and Zoriah was sure to ask pointed questions.

Bam! bam! The great door shook. Zoriah called the eunuch harem guards and directed them to the door.

As soon as they were in place, she crossed the cool stone floor to stand before Ara. "What is going on?" Her eyebrows formed a frowning V. "Where did Layla and the woman go? Who is she?"

Still fuming, Rabab removed her hijab. Her white hair was plaited tightly against her head, her mouth set in a fierce line. "This is our place. Who does that guard think he is, anyway?"

Zoriah was not to be distracted. "Ara, what is going on here? Why does the wazir seek you?"

Ara silently prayed to Allah, the merciful. "Please, Zoriah, you must help. This is no game. The wazir has set Father up for an ambush. Even now, Tahirah is riding off to prevent his capture. The Castilians are waiting in the mountains to attack. You must

197

alert the guards. Please, what I say is true," Ara's voice choked, desperate to make Zoriah understand.

She turned white but her unblinking eyes bored into Ara. "My husband rode south. Is it truly a trap?" She gave Ara a doubtful look. "How would you know?"

Ara willed her to believe. "We heard the Castilian soldiers speaking when we were hidden. Tahirah has the written proof of the ambush plot."

Zoriah nodded, no longer skeptical, and moments later she and Rabab were organizing the women and eunuch guards of the harem. Hasan was hurried off to roust the rest of the harem.

Rabab turned to fuss over the exhausted girl. "Where is Layla and...?" Her head tilted as if she were trying to place the new woman.

"We've been hiding for hours. They went to get food and rest."

Rabab gently held her for a moment. "This is too great a burden for you. You too must get some rest. My dear, you're just a girl." She looked at her objectively. "And one nigh on to collapse. I know you're worried for your father. Believe me, all will be well. Your father is no one's fool."

She patted Ara's cheek. "Now go. We have everything under control. You have done your part. Tomorrow will see no Castilians in the Alhambra."

Ara breathed a sigh. *Inshallah*, her father would survive this night, and the wazir's treacheries would be exposed. Now she needed to find the final symmetry. And hope that Suleiman would change back to himself.

She raced through the harem, looking for Layla. Time was flashing past. Rounding the corner at full tilt, she careened over Suleiman and landed head first on the floor.

Suleiman, all angles, sat hunched against the wall, well wrapped in the now foul-smelling and sweaty hijab.

"We found a glide with a vertical mirror," Layla said, pointing to a pattern low on the ground. "But it is complete."

Suleiman looked up, despair showing deep within his triangular eyes. "There are only three hours left. We may need to face that this last task cannot be done."

"We can't fail now. The Alhambra mustn't fall." Ara scanned the tiled ceiling that arched above her and whispered, "And you must be returned to your original body."

Both her friends seemed to gain hope from her words. Layla pushed away from the wall. "Let's start again."

Ara nodded. "Where have you searched so far?"

"Suleiman and I have been dodging guards and women. This is all we've found."

The trio thoroughly searched the room. Example upon example of symmetries pranced across the walls, even another glide rotation, but nowhere did they see a broken one. They scurried from room to room, nervously checking for people before they entered. Ara was sure with each new room that the spell would be broken. And in each room she noticed more and more tiny cracks in the walls.

Time edged on. Bedtime had come and gone; the girls, exhausted before, were now dragging.

They stopped to rest for what seemed only a few minutes. "What if," Layla said, "there is no broken glide rotation in the harem?"

Ara slumped to the floor "No, it must be here! At least one. We're so close. That can't be. It just can't."

She forced herself to go to the kitchen and grab some food. As she ran back to her friends, a guard standing against the wall snapped to attention.

"Sultan's child, a message came for you."

199

Ara blinked hopefully. "A message? From my father?"

"No, from the Sufi mathemagician. A messenger handed this to the guard at the door. I have been looking for you for some time."

He handed her a small piece of parchment sealed with wax. She ripped it open. The hastily scrawled message almost shouted: "Meet me in the Court of the Lions before midnight."

She looked up, confused. "Tahirah was here? Did you see her?"

"No, child of the Alhambra. Her messenger came and said it was important." He coughed uneasily. "The slave, Su'ah, did not know where you were. She is worried and scolding. You should go there now."

Ara looked again at the message, breathing a sigh of relief. Tahirah was back. Or was she? Why would she not come directly to them?

Could this be a trick, or was this the solution?

Soon it would be midnight and their time would be up. Would it be worth the danger to try? The Court of the Lions was outside the doors of the Palace of the Myrtles. How were they to get there without getting caught? All the guards were alert. She frowned. When had Tahirah sent this message? And where was she now?

"Please tell Su'ah that Layla and I are fine and not to be angry with me. We will be in bed before she knows it."

After thanking the guard again, she returned to Layla and Suleiman and made a decision. "We're going to leave the harem."

Chapter 41

Torches flickered in the light breeze. The slender, arched columns, so graceful during the day, looked foreboding in the gloom of midnight. The moon was full and bright to light their way but kept disappearing behind a veil of clouds. Stars flickered as if in warning. Ara and Layla, with Suleiman dragging behind, slunk into the courtyard. They jumped at every sound. The lions were not at their places; the bare fountain looked naked and exposed. Holding hands, the girls inched forward, carefully skirting the central fountain and keeping inside the shadow of the walls. Ara whispered in Layla ear. "This doesn't feel right. Where's Tahirah?"

A body separated itself from one of the columns. The wazir. He smiled and waved his hand. Dark, contorted shapes poured forth in fits and starts. Magic rained on the three companions, sealing all exits from the room and hobbling their movements. The arched doorways were blocked by a thick, transparent mucus that rippled and undulated.

"It's over," he said to Ara. "You've fallen right into my trap. The game has ended. Did you think a child—a girl child, at that—could best me?" He laughed, sneering at the now visible golden-maned lions pacing the room, snarling and growling, but unable to attack.

"The Alhambra's lions cannot harm me. The last spell holds." He laughed again. "There is no broken glide with a vertical mirror here. It's well hidden and far, far away. There will be no breaking the spell. Your tutor, Suleiman, will remain a goat—a roasted goat perhaps—but a goat nevertheless. Even now, your father is at the mercy of the Castilian King." Abd al-Rahmid laughed. "And you and your cousin..." He puffed himself up like a rooster. "You will serve me well as my future wives. As a kindness to you, you will remain in the Alhambra—under my protection. You should be grateful for my leniency. I'm sure with discipline you will learn to be good Muslim wives rather than palace brats."

He looked at the goat. "And Suleiman, yours will be the blood that seals the fate of the Alhambra and ends the magic forever."

Layla looked to be too afraid for tears. Suleiman's head hung in defeat. All around them they could hear cracking and groaning as the walls were pulled apart by the strain of the wazir's magic. A column broke in half, and Layla cringed.

Rigid in terror and anger but unwilling to give up, Ara glared at the wazir.

And still the lions paced.

"Shall I tell you my plan?" he boasted. "They, the proud and sure Sufis, forced me out of their school spouting of love and tolerance. But I knew. I could see the fear in their eyes.

"I was brilliant. Gifted! The best at mathemagics. But the religious instructors were old-fashioned and timid. They feared my power. I was sent away, disgraced. But I remembered and studied and planned."

He turned and paced the room as if trying to convince himself. "The Christians, those stupid Infidels, welcomed me. They believe they control me. But I have the power, not them."

A lion, as insubstantial as the air, charged him—and passed right through. The wazir flinched. He checked himself over, then pulled himself together with a dismissive shrug. "Ha! My magic is strong. Not even the lions of Alhambra can overcome it."

Suleiman watched contemplatively, a pensive look now upon his goat face, defeat no longer riding him.

Ara gritted her teeth with desperation and fury. The wazir was raving. Here was a man who had abandoned Allah, in His Wonderment, to walk alone. She shivered. How lost he must be without Allah and his comfort. Sympathy rose up unasked, and to her surprise she felt a loosening of his control over her. Deep within, she remembered she was the daughter of the sultan and of a mathemagician. She had the answer to this puzzle.

She glanced at her cousin. Incomprehension had lessened in Layla's eyes, no longer dazzled by the wazir's power. Suleiman's head was still down, but the stubbornness of a goat is not to be ignored. Ara thought she heard him whisper, "The last lesson."

The lions roared as they restlessly paced across the room. The wazir continued with a sneer. "So much for the power of the Alhambra lions," he said scornfully. "They are helpless."

Ara watched them closely before leaning to whisper in her cousin's ear. Layla nodded and let go of her hand.

The wazir chortled. "Time is on my side. Such a few minutes left before the Alhambra is delivered into my hands."

Layla edged slowly away from Ara. A clatter of feet and shouting roused Abd al-Rahmid from his self-congratulations. The sultan, Layla's father, Tahirah and her father's private guards pounded on the magically-sealed arched doorways. Ara heard her father calling to her in the midst of the assault on the doors. Through the slick of magic, she could see Tahirah pressing her hand against one door, trying to break though. Her worried eyes concentrated on the girls, and Ara felt a sigh breathe confidence in her.

The wazir frowned, pulling his sword out from the scabbard. "An unexpected annoyance. The Infidels couldn't take care of so trifling a problem, even though I placed the sultan in their hands. That Sufi witch must have aided him. No matter. They can't enter. My magic is binding." He looked back at the girls and his frown deepened. The sword hung loosely from his hand.

Ara continued, quietly stepping away from Layla, and swallowed the bubble of her rage before speaking. "You are right. It was childish of us to think we could win against one so learned and skilled. We are less than worthy of your notice—two girls and a goat. It was foolish to go against your strength and power."

He gave her a suspicious look before scoffing. "What's this? A change of heart? The sultan's daughter concedes a struggle she could never win?"

She doggedly avoided glancing at Layla and kept her attention on the wazir as she slowly slid farther away from her cousin. The steady splash from the fountain reminded her that time was escaping.

A translation, she thought, *I'm moving like a translation.* A loud groan reverberated in the room as an arched column cracked to her right.

Suleiman remained still, tiny black hooves riveted in place, tension and determination contained in his compact body. He tucked his head down a bit more, and the moonlight reflected off the tips of his horns.

Ara took another step away from Layla, then answered. "Not a change of heart. I acted as a child, unknowing of your power. Not sensing the futility of my effort."

Layla, after a number of terror-stricken looks at the wazir, slid away step by step, putting yet more distance between herself and Ara.

The wazir's expression hardened into arrogance. "You should beg my forgiveness." He raised the sword up. "You wasted much of my time and caused me to lose face with the Christians." His face turned red remembering, and he trembled with rage. "The blood of Suleiman will complete my magic."

Two more columns snapped. The lions roared again. The wazir's gaze flickered to them as if to reassure himself of their impotence before relocking on Ara.

Layla once more sidled away from her cousin. The lions snarled at the wazir and passed by Layla, giving her an approving nod. Fear crossed her face. She gulped, but she said, her voice barely audible, "Abd al-Rahmid?"

He whirled at the sound. "What? Does the mouse speak?"

Layla gulped, then said in a whisper, "I...I just thought that I would—I thought—" White with fear, she began humming the gypsy tune and, shakily at first, started the movements of a dance.

The wazir wrinkled his forehead, startled.

Ara signaled, quickly catching the attention of her lion. He snarled and padded to stand before her. She whispered in his ear.

The wazir spun around at that, and the lion drifted away. "Don't play your children's games here." He turned back to Layla with an evil grin. "You'll dance for me later, don't worry."

He'd only been distracted for a few moments. Ara hoped it would be enough.

Behind him, the lions gathered. At their thundering roar, the wazir whipped around. The twelve lions were lining up, one by one in two rows. The last lion stood facing forward, out of line, looking to Ara. A broken symmetry, created by the magic of the Alhambra lions.

Guessing their plan, the wazir blanched and sprang toward her.

She waved her lion into place.

Suleiman, head down, horns forward, charged the wazir.

Ara observed the loveliest of symmetries—twelve stone lions in a row, lion facing lion, then two again but a glide away, until all twelve lined up, creating a perfect glide with a vertical mirror. Then the goat rammed the wazir, knocked the sword out of his hand, and the two collided in a pile near her feet.

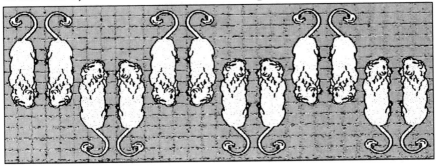

Goat and Wazir rolled across the floor in a desperate struggle. Layla screamed. The wazir's hands were clutched around the goat's neck, but the change had begun. His magic was dissolving. Lions roared over and over, their voices rising in fury. Tahirah's low call of power came from the door. Guards crashed through the entrances, and the sultan's urgent commands were heard over the din. Mouths agape, the girls watched the tumbling bodies on the floor; Suleiman's horns disappearing, his body lengthening, hooves flattening into feet. The two opponents tangled while fur crumbled into vapor. And still they fought.

A gasp rose from the guards. "It's Suleiman," one man shouted. Suleiman reared back and with his clenched fist struck a punishing blow. The wazir's head slammed against the fountain, and he slumped onto the floor.

Silence enveloped the group.

Suleiman, human once again but naked as the day he was born, stared at the motionless body of the wazir, then at himself. He blushed a bright red and, seizing a small floor rug, dove behind a pillar. The wazir's sword lay useless beside him upon the cold stone.

The spell broken, the lions were now visible to all, no longer translucent but made of fur, muscle and bone. Layla ran to her father and hid her face in his caftan. The sultan, a smear of blood across his cheek, strode across the floor to encircle Ara in his arms. The guards clattered behind and circled protectively around the sultan, his brother and the girls.

Shoulders high and heads lowered, twelve lions moved to surround the downed wazir. He opened his eyes and, with a groan, rolled slowly to his side. As the guards moved to arrest him, the lions bared their teeth, preparing to defend their prey. Still dazed from the blow, he shook his head and recoiled, cowering and covering his face at the sight of thrashing tails and snapping jaws.

Standing protectively before Ara, the sultan ordered the guards to move back. Layla's father held them steady, glancing down at his daughter in undisguised relief. While two of the lions snarled in defiance at the guards, the others moved in on the wazir. He screamed as they grabbed his arms and shoulders in their powerful jaws, pulling him toward the enormous wooden doors of the Hall of the Abencerrajes. He cried out again, this time to the sultan, pleading for clemency. Tahirah stood with her head bowed in prayer; the sultan's face was tight with misery and anger.

The wazir's screams became louder and shriller as he writhed against the lions' grip, but they pulled him step by step toward the Fountain of the Abencerrajes. Swords out, the guards stood their ground, glancing occasionally toward Layla's father for directives. Not one of them had ever seen the stone lions alive. Layla's father gently handed Layla to Tahirah and faced the lions.

Four lions acted as rear-guards; their glowing eyes watched the crowd as they shouldered the doors closed. The doors thudded shut, muffling the wazir's screams.

In answer to the unspoken questions, the sultan proclaimed, "He is theirs. The lions are the guardians of the Alhambra. They have been ensorcelled and the Alhambra threatened. Payment is due." He closed his eyes as if to ward off the pain of the wazir's betrayal and spoke so softly Ara almost missed it. "For myself, I would pardon him. But I have a duty to my people."

She peered up from the safety of her father's embrace as Layla whispered. "What's going to happen? What are they going to do?"

From behind the doors came a gurgling scream. Then there was silence, and the water flowing from the Hall of the Abencerrajes ran red. All around, the Alhambra's columns repaired themselves. The cracks in the walls sealed.

The sultan continued to hold Ara, pity etched on his face. "The Alhambra's lions bestow justice, not compassion. They see into the hearts of men and act accordingly."

He bowed his head. "It is a sad end for a man who once had much to recommend him. Now he is in Allah's hands."

As if nothing had happened, eleven lions suddenly appeared, stone-like again in their original places around the fountain. One space remained unfilled. The twelfth lion approached, dragging the wazir's caftan. He drew it through the fountain and, when he pulled it out, the blood disappeared and the material appeared pristine and dry. The lion set it before the sultan, who pushed Ara behind him into the capable hands of Tahirah.

The lion growled. "Your loyal employee no longer has fur. He has need of clothes."

The sultan bowed, equal to equal, before carefully accepting the caftan from the lion's jaws. "It is true. My deepest thanks go to you, your pride, and to Suleiman. You have done a great service to me and all of Granada."

He considered the robe for a long moment before walking to the pillar behind which Suleiman hid, in his nakedness. The tension in the sultan's body slowly dissipated as he looked at his slave. "Suleiman, might I offer you this to clothe you. Tahirah has told me of your...changes. By your selfless acts, you protected my daughter from the wazir, not once but many times. You have proved yourself loyal, brave, and resourceful, and I have need of a new advisor. I hope you will agree to wear this."

Suleiman quickly clutched the robe, covering himself. "Sire, you honor me more deeply than I deserve or need. I will accept this to cover myself, but I require no other reward than the safety of you and your family. It is my duty to protect the Nazrids."

Tahirah stepped forward, "Suleiman, take it. This was meant to be. You have the courage, learning and training to be a great advisor. You must trust yourself and your sultan."

Ara whispered, "Please, Suleiman. Father needs you."

He smiled at his charge as he stepped forth, now cloaked from head to toe. "Ah, my student. But who will take on the responsibility of your training, child?"

The sultan interposed. "Tahirah, as you know, has been filling in these last few weeks." He turned to the woman comforting the two girls. "I know you have other responsibilities, but would you consider staying with us longer? Granada could use a skilled mathemagician and poetess."

Tahirah lifted her head, her eyes pained. "Would that I could, but my duty to Allah pulls me from place to place. Yet I am saddened that I must leave. It is late, and there are tasks that I must complete before this evening can be put aside. Go, rest. Let us think on this further when the day breaks."

Chapter 42

After all had left the room, Tahirah stilled her being, sheltering herself within a prayer.

The Alhambra was almost healed. The palace whispered to her and called her name. One final task to do. No longer did it shun her.

The lions were back in their places but alert and waiting, claws and teeth prepared for any intruder. Their thoughts swirled around the room, and she had to hold her mind tightly closed against the images of fangs and claws that radiated from the fountain.

The doors to the Hall of the Abencerrajes remained closed. She knew what waited for her there. She reached deep inside herself and found...Allah. Peace and harmony flooded her being. Strength to deal with the ordeal to come.

Slowly, she walked over to the doors. She felt it even before she touched them: pain, torment. The echo of a soul in horror of itself. She took a deep breath, grabbed hold of the door and pulled. The huge door creaked open, admitting her like an old friend. It was a small room, not suited to this kind of pain. A place meant for laughter and joy. Here was where the final healing of the Alhambra had to take place. She closed the door behind her.

Breathing was hard, and the agony of the evening rang in her ears and pulsed in the stone beneath her fingertips. She knew the wazir was no longer there, no longer in pain. But his memories lingered and clawed at the walls. With deliberate steps, she began the process of cleansing the room and completing the healing of the Alhambra. She retraced patterns with their magical symmetries into the walls. The Alhambra listened and breathed in the knowledge using the patterns as a structure from which to repair damage.

Tahirah placed her hands flat on the stone floor and felt the remaining symmetries heal, one after another throughout the Alhambra, as the magnificent building incorporated the mathematics into its foundations. With each healing, she felt her closeness to Allah and rejoiced in the wonder of her Sufi mathemagic schooling. And with each healing, the echo of the wazir's pain and treachery lessened.

High above, moonlight illuminated the symmetry of the many windows set in geometric positions around a center top. As she stared, mesmerized by the light, it splintered and fractured. But this time, symmetries upon perfect symmetries danced before her mind's eye, lit by the moon and the stars.

Allah had granted her a blessing beyond her wildest imaginings. Mathematics as she had never seen it swirled before her. Symmetries flashed before her eyes and replicated themselves again and again across the ceiling. Deep into the bones of the Alhambra, she followed them. Her mind delighted at the wonders. Patterns so small that her mind could hardly grasp what she was seeing. The configuration of a future world she could but guess at, and all symmetries. Symmetries within symmetries, smaller than one could see, all part of the force which tied it together. Not to be understood in her lifetime, nor in a lifetime of lifetimes, but eventually in a land and time unknown to her or any of the wisest of the wise. A gift of knowledge she could never share.

Exhausted, she lay on her back, reveling in the oneness with the Alhambra and Allah, and gazed upwards at the ceiling into the comforting dark of the sky.

Chapter 43

Su'ah shook Ara awake. "You weren't playing with beet juice again, were you? The channels of the Lion Court ran blood red, or so say the whisperings of the servants." Her voice was laced with awe. "A guard told Maryam the stone lions came to life and killed the wazir."

She was quiet for a minute. "Do you know what really happened?"

Ara opened her eyes, still blurred with sleep, and sat up. Layla lay unmoving, watching them. "Su'ah," she was solemn. "The lions did come to life. Honestly, as Allah is my witness. The wazir sent Father into a trap, but Tahirah went to warn him. And then Layla and I went into the Court of the Lions and the wazir was there and Suleiman and they fought...."

"Suleiman's back?" Su'ah's eyes ratcheted to her forehead.

Ara smiled. "Yes, he is back." A weight had been lifted off her shoulders. Suleiman was human again. The palace was safe. Father was unharmed. All was back to normal.

Normal? Ara frowned, puzzled. Why did that bother her? Granada was a wonderful place to live, and the Alhambra the most beautiful of the beautiful. But Tahirah was leaving, and Ara didn't know if she would ever return.

Maybe Tahirah would stay; Father had invited her, after all. She couldn't imagine life with Tahirah gone.

At a muffled squeak from Layla, Ara turned to see a shimmer of light dance across the carpet. Su'ah gasped and sat down on the bed as the light congealed into the outline of a lion. Before their eyes, Ara's lion slowly materialized on the red and blue carpet. Golden stars twinkled and disappeared as he solidified. Su'ah looked near to fainting, her hand on her heart.

Layla scrambled out of bed to comfort her. But Ara leapt up and threw her arms around the huge tawny beast.

"I knew you'd come back." She buried her face in the thick mane.

The lion purred.

Ara sat upright. "What happened last night after we left? Are Suleiman and Tahirah and Father truly all right?"

The lion stretched his huge paws out until they touched Su'ah's loom. "Suleiman identified his last lessons, stubbornness and resourcefulness. They proved useful, did they not?" He bared his teeth in a cat-like grin. "He and the sultan spoke long into the night. Suleiman finally agreed to take on the wazir's cloak. Your father has a few bruises from routing his enemies." He snorted, and his teeth gleamed in a grin. "The Castilians now need to barter with him for the men they lost when your father captured them last night."

Ara nodded, "And Tahirah?"

He snorted. "She is a Sufi, restless and always on the path to spiritual awareness. Their roads are paved, not in glory, but in duty."

He collected himself and rose, towering over her. "You are the one I call on now."

"Me?" Ara exclaimed, thinking she must have heard wrongly.

"The power of Granada fades and that of the Christians grows. Mohammad's tolerance of different religions is used against us. Our sultans, like your father, have been wise and kind rulers, but it is not enough. Though we have grown rich in mathematics and science, even that will not defend the walls of the Alhambra. We are not welcome here. We will be forced out eventually, back to the deserts and plains of my kind. So now it's up to us, you and me."

"What do you mean?"

"You and I are bonded, child. Our fates woven together from your birth."

"Truly?"

213

"Yes. For each generation in the Alhambra, one child and one lion are joined. I am the last of the lions to choose a life bond."

She sat back on her heels, startled. The lion was truly hers, connected by magic. "You chose? Father has many children; why did you choose me?"

"In each generation there is a trait that has been necessary for the survival of Granada. A trait that is foremost in the human they bond to. In the past, my brothers' qualities have been in much need. Justice and Wisdom have linked many times; Courage and Vigilance also. My brother Reason bonded with your father. But my nature has never been needed." He sniffed at the flowers sitting in a vase. "Until this generation and you."

Ara shook her head slightly, though she waited for him to continue.

Purring again, the lion licked her with his rough tongue. "You are the beginning of the end. A start of a new time. Our ways are being threatened by those with a narrowness of spirit—those with a disdain for learning, and those who fear change. Not only among the Christians but also among our own people."

"But I'm just a girl."

"Yes, but a curious one. And curious girls grow into knowledgeable women. The lion roars, but the lioness rules. You embrace change, yet respect our culture. Let learning and peace remain part of who you are." Silver motes danced around him as he started fading once again. "Remember."

"What is your name?" Ara called after him, desperate. "You never told me your name."

He grinned. "My name is Curiosity. And you, my curious friend, and those like you, are the hope for our future."

Appendices

Glossary of Terms

Al-Andaluse, name of Islamic Spain pre-1500

Alhambra, The Red Palace. The palace of the Nazrid Kings in the Country of Granada

Alhamdulillah, praise be to Allah

Allah, God

Aragon, a country north of Granada, now part of Spain

Baklava, an Arabic dessert made with nuts and honey wrapped up in a flaky dough

Bedouin, a nomadic tribe of Arabs from northern Africa

Berbers, a tribe of people from northern Africa. Only blue-eyed race of Africans

Bismillah, in the name of God

Black Death, a plague that wiped out almost a quarter of the European world around 1350

Caftan, a long tunic

Caravan, a company of merchants traveling together

Castile, a country north of Granada, now part of Spain

Childbed fever, an infection of the reproductive system following childbirth

Concubine, a status of women in the harem, not married to the sultan, who also bear his children

Court of the Lions, a courtyard in the Palace of the Court of the Lions, surrounded by rooms on every side. Twelve lions support a central fountain. The original centerpiece of the fountain is no longer there. It was removed in the 1500's.

Crusades, multiple wars fought between the Christians and the Arabs over the holy lands

Emir, Arab prince, governor or commander

Ewer, a pitcher or container for liquids

Eunuch, a neutered male who worked in the harems

Five pillars of Islam: prayer, fasting, pilgrimage, almsgiving and the remembrance of God

Generalife, the summer palace of the Alhambra

Gilded Court, a courtyard in the Palace of the Myrtles

Granada, the name of the Islamic country in southern Spain
between 800 and 1492. It was also the name of the capital
city in the Kingdom of Granada
Hall of the Abencerrajes, room off the south side of the Court of
the Lions
Hall of the Ambassadors, the throne room in the Palace of the
Myrtles where the sultan received important visitors
Hall of the Kings, room on the eastern side of the Court of the
Lions
Hall of the Two Sisters, room on the north side of the Court of
the Lions
Harem, a protected place where the women and children lived. A
cloistered environment
Hijab, veil worn by Muslim women outside of their private
lodging out of modesty
Infidels, nonbelievers of the Islamic religion
Inshallah, if Allah wills
Islamic Spain, that part of Spain that was under Islamic control
before 1492
Jerusalem, the holy city for three religions, Islam, Judaism and
Christianity
Justice Gate, one of the four main gates of the Alhambra
Khanqa, a Sufi hospice
Mirador de Lindaraja, a room in the Alhambra (mirror of the
Lindaraja) off the Hall of Two Sisters
Mohammad, the spiritual founder of the Islamic religion
Mosque, religious building for Muslims
Muezzin, the person who gives the call to prayer
Navarre, a country in Spain near the French border during the
1400's
Nazrid, name of the family of rulers that controlled Granada
during the early middle ages
Palace of the Lions, one of the palaces in the Alhambra. One
hundred and twenty-four peristyles are in the courtyard

Palace of the Myrtles, one of the palaces in the Alhambra, joined
    together with the Palace of the Lions after the expulsion of
    the Muslims in 1492
Palace of the Partal, a group of buildings in the Alhambra where
    guests were frequently housed
Patio de la Acequia, a beautiful courtyard in the Generalife
People of the Book, Christians
Peristyles, tall narrow columns
Raptor, a bird of prey
Red Palace, the English translation of the name Alhambra
Rumi, a famous Sufi Arabic poet of the eleventh century
Saracens, a north African tribe
Scheherazade, a famous heroine of Arabic stories
Sierra Nevada, the mountain range in the south of Spain
Sitti, a female title of respect
Sufi, a mystic religious order of Islam
Sultan, a Muslim ruler or monarch
Tasbih, a necklace worn and used similar to a rosary
The Book of the Thousand and One Nights, the book of stories
    told through the voice of Scheherazade. Aladdin and his lamp
    is one of the better-known stories from the book
Toledo, a city in Castilian Spain once under Islamic control
Ululating, a high wavering sound made with the voice and
    tongue to indicate joy or sorrow
Vega, the great plains of southern Spain
Wazir, the office of Minister or Advisor (as in a minister of
    government)

Glossary of Names

Abn al-Humam, Layla's Father, Commander of the Army and brother of the sultan

Abd al-Rahmid, Wazir

Ara, a girl of the harem. Daughter of the sultan

Dananir, fourth wife of the sultan

Enrique, son of the Lady Theresa

Fatima, Zoriah's grandmother. One of the women living in the harem

Hasan, a young boy who lives in the harem

Lady Anna, visiting woman from the north of Spain

Lady Catalina, visiting woman from the north of Spain

Lady Theresa, visiting woman from the north of Spain

Layla, Ara's cousin

Maryam, Layla's mother

Rabab, Ara's Great Aunt, who also lives in the harem

Sara, young girl in the harem

Sister Helena, nun from the north of Spain

Sister Mary, nun from the north of Spain

Su'ah, a Saracen slave

Suleiman, a palace slave who has risen to the job of harem tutor

Sultan, Muhammad VII, father of Ara

Tahirah, famous Sufi mathemagician

Thana, second wife of the sultan's brother, Abn al-Humam

Zoriah, head wife of the sultan

Stone Lions

Loyalty	Strength
Vigilance	Prudence
Justice	Discipline
Wisdom	Courage
Endurance	Patience
Reason	Curiosity

Symmetry Summary

Band symmetry: seven symmetries that form a one-dimensional pattern (a row or band) and seventeen wallpaper symmetries (two-dimensional) have been used in art and architecture for almost as long as people have created art and architecture.

Recently, three-dimensional symmetry was discovered to be important in many areas of science; in particular, crystallography and particle science. This book is an introduction to band symmetry (one-dimensional symmetry).

There are seven possible band symmetries

1.Vertical Reflection

A symmetry family with a vertical reflection. There is no rotation and no horizontal reflection.
Bilateral Symmetry is included in this group. Two of the vertical lines are shown here with arrows.

2. Horizontal Reflection

A symmetry family with a horizontal reflection. There is no rotation and no vertical reflection. The single horizontal line is shown above.

3. Double reflection

A symmetry family that has two reflections, one over a horizontal line and over a vertical line. It does rotate and it looks the same upside down as right side up. The single horizontal line plus two of many possible vertical lines of reflection are shown above.

4. Translation

An asymmetrical shape with no reflection and no rotation. It moves by translation or sliding. No vertical or horizontal lines are possible.

5. Rotation

An asymmetrical object that rotates around a point. There is no reflection. Three of the points of rotation are shown above with dots.

6. Glide reflection

An asymmetric object with a glide. No vertical mirror, does not rotate. The object glides (the triangle shows the first glide) and then reflects. The horizontal line is shown as a single glide.

7. Glide with a vertical mirror

A symmetric object (the vertical mirror) that glides. It also can be seen to rotate. The object reflects, creating the double triangle, then it glides (as shown by the double triangle) and then it reflects. The horizontal line is shown. This symmetry can also rotate. Two of the points of rotation are shown with dots.

<u>And Four Motions</u>

Reflection (mirror or flip), the image flips over a horizontal or vertical line

Rotation, the image turns around a fixed point

Translation (Slide), the image moves along the row one space

Glide reflection, the image moves along the row one space and then flips over a horizontal line

The Alhambra Palace

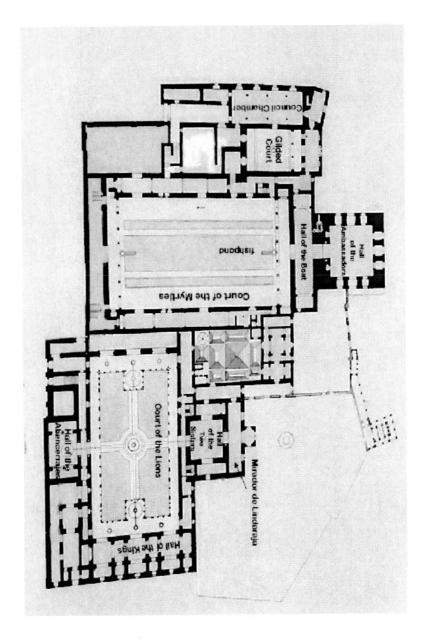

The Alhambra

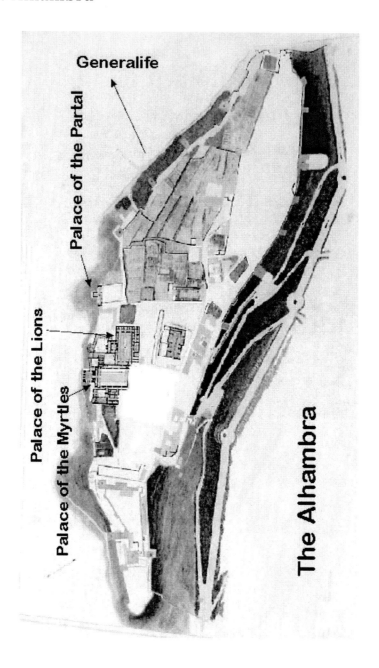

Generalife · Palace of the Partal · Palace of the Lions · Palace of the Myrtles · The Alhambra

224

Al Andalusia Circa 1390's

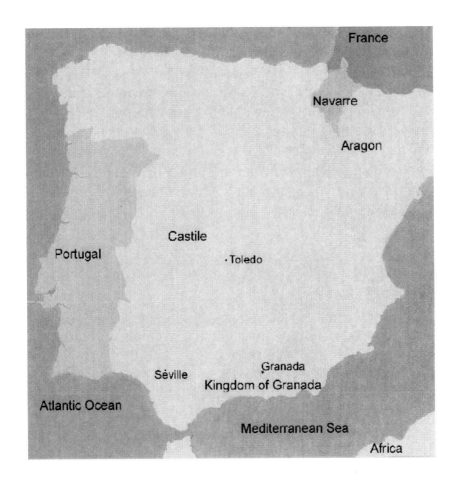

About the Author

For many years, I supported myself as a systems analyst, but now I've focused myself as a dedicated dilettante of art.

I bake seriously and garden. Reading is my passion. I read fantasy (and any other written material put near me) and have walls of books in my house.

Not so long ago, my life centered around Morris and short sword dancing. I started writing around the time I ended my fifty bell dancing habit.

During the last fifteen years, I have belonged to SCBWI (Society of Children's Book Writers and Illustrators) and have been active within the group.

My golden retriever and my husband keep me active, hiking and roaming the hills.

CPSIA information can be obtained at www.ICGtesting.com
Printed in the USA
LVOW08s2015180215

427448LV00018B/897/P